The Virgin and the Gipsy

David Herbert Lawrence

CHAPTER 1

When the vicar's wife went off with a young and penniless man the scandal knew no bounds. Her two little girls were only seven and nine years old respectively. And the vicar was such a good husband. True, his hair was grey. But his moustache was dark, he was handsome, and still full of furtive passion for his unrestrained and beautiful wife.

Why did she go? Why did she burst away with such an *éclat* of revulsion, like a touch of madness?

Nobody gave any answer. Only the pious said she was a bad woman. While some of the good women kept silent. They knew.

The two little girls never knew. Wounded, they decided that it was because their mother found them negligible.

The ill wind that blows nobody any good swept away the vicarage family on its blast. Then lo and behold! the vicar, who was somewhat distinguished as an essayist and a controversialist, and whose case had aroused sympathy among the bookish men, received the living of Papplewick. The Lord had tempered the wind of misfortune with a rectorate in the north country.

The rectory was a rather ugly stone house down by the river Papple, before you come into the village. Further on, beyond where the road crosses the stream, were the big old stone cotton-mills, once driven by water. The road curved uphill, into the bleak stone streets of the village.

The vicarage family received decided modification, upon its transference into the rectory. The vicar, now the rector, fetched up his old mother and his sister, and a brother from the city. The two little girls had a very different milieu from the old home.

The rector was now forty-seven years old, he had displayed an intense and not very dignified grief after the flight of his wife. Sympathetic ladies had stayed him from suicide. His hair was almost white, and he had a wild-eyed, tragic look. You had only to look at him, to know how dreadful it all was, and how he had been wronged.

Yet somewhere there was a false note. And some of the ladies, who had sympathised most profoundly with the vicar, secretly rather disliked the rector. There was a certain furtive self-righteousness about him, when all was said and done.

The little girls, of course, in the vague way of children, accepted the family verdict. Granny, who was over seventy and whose sight was failing, became the central figure in the house. Aunt Cissie, who was over forty, pale, pious, and gnawed by an inward worm, kept house. Uncle Fred, a stingy and grey-faced man of forty, who just lived dingily for himself, went into town every day. And the rector, of course, was the most important person, after Granny.

They called her The Mater. She was one of those physically vulgar, clever old bodies who had got her own way all her life by buttering the weaknesses of her men-folk. Very quickly she took her cue. The rector still "loved" his delinquent wife, and would "love her" till he died. Therefore hush! The rector's feeling was sacred. In his heart was enshrined the pure girl he had wedded and worshipped.

Out in the evil world, at the same time, there wandered a disreputable woman who had betrayed the rector and abandoned his little children. She was now yoked to a young and despicable man, who no doubt would bring her the degradation she deserved. Let this be clearly understood, and then hush! For in the pure loftiness of the rector's heart still bloomed the pure white snowflower of his young bride. This white snowflower did not wither. That other creature, who had gone off with that despicable young man, was none of his affair.

The Mater, who had been somewhat diminished and insignificant as a widow in a small house, now climbed into the chief arm-chair in the rectory, and planted her old bulk firmly again. She was not going to be dethroned. Astutely she gave a sigh of homage to the rector's fidelity to the pure white snowflower, while she pretended to disapprove. In sly reverence for her son's great love, she spoke no word against that nettle which flourished in the evil world, and which had once been called Mrs. Arthur Saywell. Now, thank heaven, having married again, she was no more Mrs. Arthur Saywell. No woman bore the rector's name. The pure white snow-flower bloomed *in perpetuum,* without nomenclature. The family even thought of her as She-who-was-Cynthia.

All this was water on the Mater's mill. It secured her against Arthur's ever marrying again. She had him by his feeblest weakness, his skulking self-love. He had married an imperishable white snowflower. Lucky man! He had been injured! Unhappy man! He had suffered. Ah, what a heart of love! And he had—forgiven! Yes, the white snowflower was forgiven. He even had made provision in his will for her, when that other scoundrel—But hush! Don't even *think* too near to that horrid nettle in the rank outer world! She-who-was-Cynthia. Let the white snowflower bloom inaccessible on the heights of the past. The present is another story.

The children were brought up in this atmosphere of cunning self-sanctification and of unmentionability. They too, saw the snowflower on inaccessible heights. They too knew that it was throned in lone splendour aloft their lives, never to be touched.

At the same time, out of the squalid world sometimes would come a rank, evil smell of selfishness and degraded lust, the smell of that awful nettle, She-who-was-Cynthia. This nettle actually contrived, at intervals, to get a little note through to her girls, her children. And at this the silver-haired Mater shook inwardly with hate. For if She-who-was-Cynthia ever came back, there wouldn't be much left of the Mater. A secret gust of hate went from the old granny to the girls, children of that foul nettle of lust, that Cynthia who had had such an affectionate contempt for the Mater.

Mingled with all this, was the children's perfectly distinct recollection of their real home, the Vicarage in the south, and their glamorous but not very dependable mother, Cynthia. She had made a great glow, a flow of life, like a swift and dangerous sun in the home, forever coming and going. They always associated her presence with brightness, but also with danger; with glamour, but with fearful selfishness.

Now the glamour was gone, and the white snowflower, like a porcelain wreath, froze on its grave. The danger of instability, the peculiarly *dangerous* sort of selfishness, like lions and tigers, was also gone. There was now a complete stability, in which one could perish safely.

But they were growing up. And as they grew, they became more definitely confused, more actively puzzled. The Mater, as she grew older, grew blinder. Somebody had to lead her about. She did not get up till towards midday. Yet blind or bed-ridden, she held the house.

Besides, she wasn't bed-ridden. Whenever the *men* were present, the Mater was in her throne. She was too cunning to court neglect. Especially as she had rivals.

Her great rival was the younger girl, Yvette. Yvette had some of the vague, careless blitheness of She-who-was-Cynthia. But this one was more docile. Granny perhaps had caught her in time. Perhaps!

The rector adored Yvette, and spoiled her with a doting fondness; as much as to say: am I not a soft-hearted, indulgent old boy! He liked to have weaknesses to a hair's-breadth. She knew them, this opinion of himself, and the Mater knew his and she traded on them by turning them into decorations for him, for his character. He wanted, in his own eyes, to have a fascinating character, as women want to have fascinating dresses. And the Mater cunningly put beauty-spots over his defects and deficiencies. Her mother-love gave her the clue to his weaknesses, and she hid them for him with decorations. Whereas She-who-was-Cynthia—! But don't mention *her,* in this connection. In her eyes, the rector was almost humpbacked and an idiot.

The funny thing was, Granny secretly hated Lucille, the elder girl, more than the pampered Yvette. Lucille, the uneasy and irritable, was more conscious of being under Granny's power, than was the spoilt and vague Yvette.

On the other hand, Aunt Cissie hated Yvette. She hated her very name. Aunt Cissie's life had been sacrificed to the Mater, and Aunt Cissie knew it, and the Mater knew she knew it. Yet as the years went on, it became a convention. The convention of Aunt Cissie's sacrifice was accepted by everybody, including the self-same Cissie. She prayed a good deal about it. Which also showed that she had her own private feelings somewhere, poor thing. She had ceased to be Cissie, she had lost her life and her sex. And now, she was creeping towards fifty, strange green flares of rage would come up in her, and at such times, she was insane.

But Granny held her in her power. And Aunt Cissie's one object in life was to look after The Mater.

Aunt Cissie's green flares of hellish hate would go up against all young things, sometimes. Poor thing, she prayed and tried to obtain forgiveness from heaven. But what had been done to her, *she* could not forgive, and the vitriol would spurt in her veins sometimes.

It was not as if the Mater were a warm, kindly soul. She wasn't. She only seemed it, cunningly. And the fact dawned gradually on the girls. Under her old-fashioned lace cap, under her silver hair, under the black silk of her stout, forward-bulging body, this old woman had a cunning heart, seeking forever her own female power. And through the weakness of the unfresh, stagnant men she had bred, she kept her power, as her years rolled on, seventy to eighty, and from eighty on the new lap, towards ninety.

For in the family there was a whole tradition of "loyalty"; loyalty to one another, and especially to the Mater. The Mater, of course, was the pivot of the family. The family was her own extended ego. Naturally she covered it with her power. And her sons and daughters, being weak and disintegrated, naturally were loyal. Outside the family, what was there for them but danger and insult and ignominy? Had not the rector experienced it, in his marriage. So now, caution! Caution and loyalty, fronting the world! Let there be as much hate and friction *inside* the family, as you like. To the outer world, a stubborn fence of unison.

CHAPTER 2

But it was not until the girls finally came home from school, that they felt the full weight of Granny's dear old hand on their lives. Lucille was now nearly twenty-one, and Yvette nineteen. They had been to a good girls' school, and had had a finishing year in Lausanne, and were quite the usual thing, tall young creatures with fresh, sensitive faces and bobbed hair and young-manly, deuce-take-it manners.

"What's so awfully *boring* about Papplewick," said Yvette, as they stood on the Channel boat watching the grey, grey cliffs of Dover draw near, "is that there are no *men* about. Why doesn't Daddy have some good old sports for friends? As for Uncle Fred, he's the limit!"

"Oh, you never know what will turn up," said Lucille, more philosophic.

"You jolly well know what to expect," said Yvette. "Choir on Sundays, and I hate mixed choirs. Boys' voices are *lovely,* when there are no women. And Sunday School and Girls' Friendly, and socials, all the dear old souls that enquire after Granny! Not a decent young fellow for miles."

"Oh I don't know!" said Lucille. "There's always the Framleys. And you know Gerry Somercotes *adores* you."

"Oh but I *hate* fellows who adore me!" cried Yvette, turning up her sensitive nose. "They *bore* me. They hang on like lead."

"Well what *do* you want, if you can't stand being adored? *I* think it's perfectly all right to be adored. You know you'll never marry them, so why not let them go on adoring, if it amuses them."

"Oh but I *want* to get married," cried Yvette.

"Well in that case, let them go on adoring you till you find one that you can *possibly* marry."

"I never should, that way. Nothing puts me off like an adoring fellow. They *bore* me so! They make me feel beastly."

"Oh, so they do me, if they get pressing. But at a distance, I think they're rather nice."

"I should like to fall *violently* in love."

"Oh, very likely! I shouldn't! I should hate it. Probably so would you, if it actually happened. After all, we've got to settle down a bit, before we know what we want."

"But don't you *hate* going back to Papplewick?" cried Yvette, turning up her young sensitive nose.

"No, not particularly. I suppose we shall be rather bored. I wish Daddy would get a car. I suppose we shall have to drag the old bikes out. Wouldn't you like to get up to Tansy Moor?"

"Oh, *love* it! Though it's an awful strain, shoving an old push-bike up those hills."

The ship was nearing the grey cliffs. It was summer, but a grey day. The two girls wore their coats with fur collars turned up, and little *chic* hats pulled down over their ears. Tall, slender, fresh-faced, naïve, yet confident, too confident, in their school-girlish arrogance, they were so terribly English. They seemed so free, and were as a matter of fact so tangled and tied up, inside themselves. They seemed so dashing and unconventional, and were really so conventional, so, as it were, shut up indoors inside themselves. They looked like bold, tall young sloops, just slipping from the harbour, into the wide seas of life. And they were, as a matter of fact, two poor young rudderless lives, moving from one chain anchorage to another.

The rectory struck a chill into their hearts as they entered. It seemed ugly, and almost sordid, with the dank air of that middle-class, degenerated comfort which has ceased to be comfortable and has turned stuffy, unclean. The hard, stone house struck the girls as being unclean, they could not have said why. The shabby furniture seemed somehow sordid, nothing was fresh. Even the food at meals had that awful dreary sordidness which is so repulsive to a young thing coming from abroad. Roast beef and wet cabbage, cold mutton and mashed potatoes, sour pickles, inexcusable puddings.

Granny, who "loved a bit of pork," also had special dishes, beef-tea and rusks, or a small savoury custard. The grey-faced Aunt Cissie ate nothing at all. She would sit at table, and take a single lonely and naked boiled potato on to her plate. She never ate meat. So she sat in sordid durance, while the meal went on, and Granny quickly slobbered her portion—lucky if she spilled nothing on her protuberant stomach. The food was not appetising in itself: how could it be, when Aunt Cissie hated food herself, hated the fact of eating, and never could keep a maidservant for three months. The girls ate with repulsion, Lucille bravely bearing up, Yvette's tender nose showing her disgust. Only the rector, white-haired, wiped his long grey moustache with his serviette, and cracked jokes. He too was getting heavy and inert, sitting in his study all day, never taking exercise. But he cracked sarcastic little jokes all the time, sitting there under the shelter of the Mater.

The country, with its steep hills and its deep, narrow valleys, was dark and gloomy, yet had a certain powerful strength of its own. Twenty miles away was the black industrialism of the north. Yet the village of Papplewick was comparatively lonely, almost lost, the life in it stony and dour. Everything was stone, with a hardness that was almost poetic, it was so unrelenting.

It was as the girls had known: they went back into the choir, they helped in the parish. But Yvette struck absolutely against Sunday School, the Band of Hope, the Girls' Friendlies—indeed against all those functions that were conducted by determined old maids and obstinate, stupid elderly men. She avoided church duties as much as possible, and got away from the rectory whenever she could. The Framleys, a big, untidy, jolly family up at the Grange, were an enormous standby. And if anybody asked her out to a meal, even if a woman in one of the workmen's houses asked her to stay to tea, she accepted at once. In fact, she was rather thrilled. She liked talking to the working men, they had often such fine, hard heads. But of course they were in another world.

So the months went by. Gerry Somercotes was still an adorer. There were others, too, sons of farmers or mill-owners. Yvette really ought to have had a good time. She was always out to parties and dances, friends came for her in their motor-cars, and off she went to the city, to the afternoon dance in the chief hotel, or in the gorgeous new Palais de Danse, called the Pally.

Yet she always seemed like a creature mesmerised. She was never free to be quite jolly. Deep inside her worked an intolerable irritation, which she thought she *ought* not to feel, and which she hated feeling, thereby making it worse. She never understood at all whence it arose.

At home, she truly was irritable, and outrageously rude to Aunt Cissie. In fact Yvette's awful temper became one of the family by-words.

Lucille, always more practical, got a job in the city as private secretary to a man who needed somebody with fluent French and shorthand. She went back and forth every day, by the same train as Uncle Fred. But she never travelled with him, and wet or fine, bicycled to the station, while he went on foot.

The two girls were both determined that what they wanted was a really jolly social life. And they resented with fury that the rectory was, for their friends, impossible. There were only four rooms downstairs: the kitchen, where lived the two discontented maid-servants: the dark dining-room: the rector's study: and the big, "homely," dreary living-room or drawing-room. In the dining-room there was a gas fire. Only in the living-room was a good hot fire kept going. Because of course, here Granny reigned.

In this room the family was assembled. At evening, after dinner, Uncle Fred and the rector invariably played crossword puzzles with Granny.

"Now, Mater, are you ready? N blank blank blank blank W: a Siamese functionary."

"Eh? Eh? M blank blank blank blank W?"

Granny was hard of hearing.

"No Mater. Not M! N blank blank blank blank W: a Siamese functionary."

"N blank blank blank blank W: a Chinese functionary."

"SIAMESE."

"Eh?"

"SIAMESE! SIAM!"

"A Siamese functionary! Now what can that be?" said the old lady profoundly, folding her hands on her round stomach. Her two sons proceeded to make suggestions, at which she said Ah! Ah! The rector was amazingly clever at cross-word puzzles. But Fred had a certain technical vocabulary.

"This certainly is a hard nut to crack," said the old lady, when they were all stuck.

Meanwhile Lucille sat in a corner with her hands over her ears, pretending to read, and Yvette irritably made drawings, or hummed loud and exasperating tunes, to add to the family concert. Aunt Cissie continually reached for a chocolate, and her jaws worked ceaselessly. She literally lived on chocolates. Sitting in the distance, she put another into her mouth, then looked again at the parish magazine. Then she lifted her head, and saw it was time to fetch Granny's cup of Horlicks.

While she was gone, in nervous exasperation Yvette would open the window. The room was never fresh, she imagined it smelt: smelt of Granny. And Granny, who was hard of hearing, heard like a weasel when she wasn't wanted to.

"Did you open the window, Yvette? I think you might remember there are older people than yourself in the room," she said.

"It's stifling! It's unbearable! No wonder we've all of us always got colds."

"I'm sure the room is large enough, and a good fire burning." The old lady gave a little shudder. "A draught to give us all our death."

"Not a draught at all," roared Yvette. "A breath of fresh air."

The old lady shuddered again, and said:

"Indeed!"

The rector, in silence, marched to the window and firmly closed it. He did not look at his daughter meanwhile. He hated thwarting her. But she must know what's what!

The cross-word puzzles, invented by Satan himself, continued till Granny had had her Horlicks, and was to go to bed. Then came the ceremony of Goodnight! Everybody stood up. The girls went to be kissed by the blind old woman. The rector gave his arm, and Aunt Cissie followed with a candle.

But this was already nine o'clock, although Granny was really getting old, and should have been in bed sooner. But when she was in bed, she could not sleep, till Aunt Cissie came.

"You see," said Granny, "I have *never* slept alone. For fifty-four years I never slept a night without the Pater's arm round me. And when he was gone, I tried to sleep alone. But as sure as my eyes closed to sleep, my heart nearly jumped out of my body, and I lay in a palpitation. Oh, you may think what you will, but it was a fearful experience, after fifty-four years of perfect married life! I would have prayed to be taken first, but the Pater, well, no I don't think he would have been able to bear up."

So Aunt Cissie slept with Granny. And she hated it. She said *she* could never sleep. And she grew greyer and greyer, and the food in the house got worse, and Aunt Cissie had to have an operation.

But The Mater rose as ever, towards noon, and at the mid-day meal, she presided from her arm-chair, with her stomach protruding, her reddish, pendulous face, that had a sort of horrible majesty, dropping soft under the wall of her high brow, and her blue eyes peering unseeing. Her white hair was getting scanty, it was altogether a little indecent. But the rector jovially cracked his jokes to her, and she pretended to disapprove. But she was perfectly complacent, sitting in her ancient obesity, and after meals, getting the wind from her stomach, pressing her bosom with her hand as she "rifted" in gross physical complacency.

What the girls minded most was that, when they brought their young friends to the house, Granny always was there, like some awful idol of old flesh, consuming all the attention. There was only the one room for everybody. And there sat the old lady, with Aunt Cissie keeping an acrid guard over her. Everybody must be presented first to Granny: she was ready to be genial, she liked company. She had to know who everybody was, where they came from, every circumstance of their lives. And then, when she was *au fait,* she could get hold of the conversation.

Nothing could be more exasperating to the girls. "Isn't old Mrs. Saywell wonderful! She takes *such* an interest in life, at nearly ninety!"

"She does take an interest in people's affairs, if that's life," said Yvette.

Then she would immediately feel guilty. After all, it *was* wonderful to be nearly ninety, and have such a clear mind! And Granny never *actually* did anybody any harm. It was more that she was in the way. And perhaps it was rather awful to hate somebody because they were old and in the way.

Yvette immediately repented, and was nice. Granny blossomed forth into reminiscences of when she was a girl, in the little town in Buckinghamshire. She talked and talked away, and was *so* entertaining. She really *was* rather wonderful.

Then in the afternoon Lottie and Ella and Bob Framley came, with Leo Wetherell.

"Oh, come in!"—and in they all trooped to the sitting-room, where Granny, in her white cap, sat by the fire.

"Granny, this is Mr. Wetherell."

"Mr. What-did-you-say? You must excuse me, I'm a little deaf!"

Granny gave her hand to the uncomfortable young man, and gazed silently at him, sightlessly.

"You are not from our parish?" she asked him.

"Dinnington!" he shouted.

"We want to go to a picnic tomorrow, to Bonsall Head, in Leo's car. We can all squeeze in," said Ella in a low voice.

"Did you say Bonsall Head?" asked Granny.

"Yes!"

There was a blank silence.

"Did you say you were going in a car?"

"Yes! In Mr. Wetherell's."

"I hope he's a good driver. It's a very dangerous road."

"He's a *very* good driver."

"Not a very good driver?"

"Yes! He *is* a very good driver."

"If you go to Bonsall Head, I think I must send a message to Lady Louth."

Granny always dragged in this miserable Lady Louth, when there was company.

"Oh, we shan't go that way," cried Yvette.

"Which way?" said Granny. "You must go by Heanor."

The whole party sat, as Bob expressed it, like stuffed ducks, fidgeting on their chairs.

Aunt Cissie came in—and then the maid with the tea. There was the eternal and everlasting piece of bought cake. Then appeared a plate of little fresh cakes. Aunt Cissie had actually sent to the baker's.

"Tea, Mater!"

The old lady gripped the arms of her chair. Everybody rose and stood, while she waded slowly across, on Aunt Cissie's arm, to her place at table.

During tea Lucille came in from town, from her job. She was simply worn out, with black marks under her eyes. She gave a cry, seeing all the company.

As soon as the noise had subsided, and the awkwardness was resumed, Granny said:

"You have never mentioned Mr. Wetherell to me, have you, Lucille?"

"I don't remember," said Lucille.

"You can't have done. The name is strange to me."

Yvette absently grabbed another cake, from the now almost empty plate. Aunt Cissie, who was driven almost crazy by Yvette's vague and inconsiderate ways, felt the green rage fuse in her heart. She picked up her own plate, on which was the one cake she allowed herself, and said with vitriolic politeness, offering it to Yvette:

"Won't you have mine?"

"Oh, thanks!" said Yvette, starting in her angry vagueness. And with an appearance of the same insouciance, she helped herself to Aunt Cissie's cake also, adding as an afterthought: "If you're sure you don't want it."

She now had two cakes on her plate. Lucille had gone white as a ghost, bending to her tea. Aunt Cissie sat with a green look of poisonous resignation. The awkwardness was an agony.

But Granny, bulkily enthroned and unaware, only said, in the centre of the cyclone:

"If you are motoring to Bonsall Head tomorrow, Lucille, I wish you would take a message from me to Lady Louth."

"Oh!" said Lucille, giving a queer look across the table at the sightless old woman. Lady Louth was the King Charles' Head of the family, invariably produced by Granny for the benefit of visitors. "Very well!"

"She was so very kind last week. She sent her chauffeur over with a Cross-word Puzzle book for me."

"But you thanked her then," cried Yvette.

"I should like to send her a note."

"We can post it," cried Lucille.

"Oh no! I should like you to take it. When Lady Louth called last time … "

The young ones sat like a shoal of young fishes dumbly mouthing at the surface of the water, while Granny went on about Lady Louth. Aunt Cissie, the two girls knew, was still helpless, almost unconscious in a paroxysm of rage about the cake. Perhaps, poor thing, she was praying.

It was a mercy when the friends departed. But by that time the two girls were both haggard-eyed. And it was then that Yvette, looking round, suddenly saw the stony, implacable will-to-power in the old and motherly-seeming Granny. She sat there bulging backwards in her chair, impassive, her reddish, pendulous old face rather mottled, almost unconscious, but implacable, her face like a mask that hid something stony, relentless. It was the static inertia of her unsavoury power. Yet in a minute she would open her ancient mouth to find out every detail about Leo Wetherell. For the moment she was hibernating in her oldness, her agedness. But in a minute her mouth would open, her mind would flicker awake, and with her insatiable greed for life, other people's life, she would start on her quest for every detail. She was like the old toad which Yvette had watched, fascinated, as it sat on the ledge of the beehive, immediately in front of the little entrance by which the bees emerged, and which, with a demonish lightning-like snap of its pursed jaws, caught every bee as it came out to launch into the air, swallowed them one after the other, as if it could consume the whole hive-full, into its aged, bulging, purse-like wrinkledness. It had been swallowing bees as they launched into the air of spring, year after year, year after year, for generations:

But the gardener, called by Yvette, was in a rage, and killed the creature with a stone.

"'Appen tha *art* good for th' snails," he said, as he came down with the stone. "But tha 'rt none goin' ter emp'y th' bee-'ive into thy guts."

CHAPTER 3

The next day was dull and low, and the roads were awful, for it had been raining for weeks, yet the young ones set off on their trip, without taking Granny's message either. They just slipped out while she was making her slow trip upstairs after lunch. Not for anything would they have called at Lady Louth's house. That widow of a knighted doctor, a harmless person indeed, had become an obnoxity in their lives.

Six young rebels, they sat very perkily in the car as they swished through the mud. Yet they had a peaked look too. After all, they had nothing really to rebel against, any of them. They were left so very free in their movements. Their parents let them do almost entirely as they liked. There wasn't really a fetter to break, nor a prison-bar to file through, nor a bolt to shatter. The keys of their lives were in their own hands. And there they dangled inert.

It is very much easier to shatter prison bars than to open undiscovered doors to life. As the younger generation finds out, somewhat to its chagrin. True, there was Granny. But poor old Granny, you couldn't actually say to her: "Lie down and die, you old woman!" She might be an old nuisance, but she never really *did* anything. It wasn't fair to hate her.

So the young people set off on their jaunt, trying to be very full of beans. They could really do as they liked. And so, of course, there was nothing to do but sit in the car and talk a lot of criticism of other people, and silly flirty gallantry that was really rather a bore. If there had only been a few "strict orders" to be disobeyed! But nothing: beyond the refusal to carry the message to Lady Louth, of which the rector would approve, because he didn't encourage King Charles' Head either.

They sang, rather scrappily, the latest would-be comic songs, as they went through the grim villages. In the great park the deer were in groups near the road, roe deer and fallow, nestling in the gloom of the afternoon under the oaks by the road, as if for the stimulus of human company.

Yvette insisted on stopping and getting out to talk to them. The girls, in their Russian boots, tramped through the damp grass while the deer watched them with big, unfrightened eyes. The hart trotted away mildly, holding back his head, because of the weight of the horns. But the doe, balancing her big ears, did not rise from under the tree, with her half-grown young ones, till the girls were almost in touch. Then she walked lightfoot away, lifting her tail from her spotted flanks, while the young ones nimbly trotted.

"Aren't they awfully dainty and nice!" cried Yvette. "You'd wonder they could lie so cosily in this horrid wet grass."

"Well I suppose they've got to lie down *sometime*," said Lucille. "And it's *fairly* dry under the tree." She looked at the crushed grass, where the deer had lain.

Yvette went and put her hand down, to feel how it felt.

"Yes!" she said, doubtfully, "I believe it's a bit warm."

The deer had bunched again a few yards away, and were standing motionless in the gloom of the afternoon. Away below the slopes of grass and trees, beyond the swift river with its balustraded bridge, sat the huge ducal house, one or two chimneys smoking bluely. Behind it rose purplish woods.

The girls, pushing their fur collars up to their ears, dangling one long arm, stood watching in silence, their wide Russian boots protecting them from the wet grass. The great house squatted square and creamy-grey below. The deer, in little groups, were scattered under the old trees close by. It all seemed so still, so unpretentious, and so sad.

"I wonder where the Duke is now," said Ella.

"Not here, wherever he is," said Lucille. "I expect he's abroad where the sun shines."

The motor horn called from the road, and they heard Leo's voice:

"Come on boys! If we're going to get to the Head and down to Amberdale for tea, we'd better move."

They crowded into the car again, with chilled feet, and set off through the park, past the silent spire of the church, out through the great gates and over the bridge, on into the wide, damp, stony village of Woodlinkin, where the river ran. And thence, for a long time, they stayed in the mud and dark and dampness of the valley, often with sheer rock above them; the water brawling on one hand, the steep rock or dark trees on the other.

Till, through the darkness of overhanging trees, they began to climb, and Leo changed the gear. Slowly the car toiled up through the whitey-grey mud, into the stony village of Bolehill, that hung on the slope, round the old cross, with its steps, that stood where the road branched, on past the cottages whence came a wonderful smell of hot tea-cakes, and beyond, still upwards, under dripping trees and past broken slopes of bracken, always climbing. Until the cleft became shallower, and the trees finished, and the slopes on either side were bare, gloomy grass, with low dry-stone walls. They were emerging on to the Head.

The party had been silent for some time. On either side the road was grass, then a low stone fence, and the swelling curve of the hill-summit, traced with the low, dry-stone walls. Above this, the low sky.

The car ran out, under the low, grey sky, on the naked tops.

"Shall we stay a moment?" called Leo.

"Oh yes!" cried the girls.

And they scrambled out once more, to look around. They knew the place quite well. But still, if one came to the Head, one got out to look.

The hills were like the knuckles of a hand, the dales were below, between the fingers, narrow, steep, and dark. In the deeps a train was steaming, slowly pulling north: a small thing of the underworld. The noise of the engine re-echoed curiously upwards. Then came the dull, familiar sound of blasting in a quarry.

Leo, always on the go, moved quickly.

"Shall we be going?" he said. "Do we *want* to get down to Amberdale for tea? Or shall we try somewhere nearer?"

They all voted for Amberdale, for the Marquis of Grantham.

"Well, which way shall we go back? Shall we go by Codnor and over Crossbill, or shall we go by Ashbourne?"

There was the usual dilemma. Then they finally decided on the Codnor top road. Off went the car, gallantly.

They were on the top of the world, now, on the back of the fist. It was naked, too, as the back of your fist, high under heaven, and dull, heavy green. Only it was veined with a network of old stone walls, dividing the fields, and broken here and there with ruins of old lead-mines and works. A sparse stone farm bristled with six naked sharp trees. In the distance was a patch of smokey grey stone, a hamlet. In some fields grey, dark sheep fed silently, somberly. But there was not a sound nor a movement. It was the roof of England, stony and arid as any roof. Beyond, below, were the shires.

"'And see the coloured counties,'" said Yvette to herself. Here anyhow they were not coloured. A stream of rooks trailed out from nowhere. They had been walking, pecking, on a naked field that had been manured. The car ran on between the grass and stone walls of the upland lane, and the young people were silent, looking out over the far network of stone fences, under the sky, looking for the curves downward that indicated a drop to one of the underneath, hidden dales.

Ahead was a light cart, driven by a man, and trudging along at the side was a woman, sturdy and elderly, with a pack on her back. The man in the cart had caught her up, and now was keeping pace.

The road was narrow. Leo sounded the horn sharply. The man on the cart looked round, but the woman on foot only trudged steadily, rapidly forward, without turning her head.

Yvette's heart gave a jump. The man on the cart was a gipsy, one of the black, loose-bodied, handsome sort. He remained seated on his cart, turning round and gazing at the occupants of the motor-car, from under the brim of his cap. And his pose was loose, his gaze insolent in its indifference. He had a thin black moustache under his thin, straight nose, and a big silk handkerchief of red and yellow tied round his neck. He spoke a word to the woman. She stood a second, solid, to turn round and look at the occupants of the car, which had now drawn quite close. Leo honked the horn again, imperiously. The woman, who had a grey-and-white kerchief tied round her head, turned sharply, to keep pace with the cart, whose driver also had settled back, and was lifting the reins, moving his loose, light shoulders. But still he did not pull aside.

Leo made the horn scream, as he put the brakes on and the car slowed up near the back of the cart. The gipsy turned round at the din, laughing in his dark face under his dark-green cap, and said something which they did not hear, showing white teeth under the line of black moustache, and making a gesture with his dark, loose hand.

"Get out o' the way then!" yelled Leo.

For answer, the man delicately pulled the horse to a standstill, as it curved to the side of the road. It was a good roan horse, and a good, natty, dark-green cart.

Leo, in a rage, had to jam on the brake and pull up too.

"Don't the pretty young ladies want to hear their fortunes?" said the gipsy on the cart, laughing except for his dark, watchful eyes, which went from face to face, and lingered on Yvette's young, tender face.

She met his dark eyes for a second, their level search, their insolence, their complete indifference to people like Bob and Leo, and something took fire in her breast. She thought: "He is stronger than I am! He doesn't care!"

"Oh yes! let's!" cried Lucille at once.

"Oh yes!" chorused the girls.

"I say! What about the time?" cried Leo.

"Oh bother the old time! Somebody's always dragging in time by the forelock," cried Lucille.

"Well, if you don't mind *when* we get back, *I* don't!" said Leo heroically.

The gipsy man had been sitting loosely on the side of his cart, watching the faces. He now jumped softly down from the shaft, his knees a bit stiff. He was apparently a man something over thirty, and a beau in his way. He wore a sort of shooting-jacket, double-breasted, coming only to the hips, of dark green-and-black frieze; rather tight black trousers, black boots, and a dark-green cap; with the big yellow-and-red bandanna handkerchief round his neck. His appearance was curiously elegant, and quite expensive in its gipsy style. He was handsome, too, pressing in his chin with the old, gipsy conceit, and now apparently not heeding the strangers any more, as he led his good roan horse off the road, preparing to back his cart.

The girls saw for the first time a deep recess in the side of the road, and two caravans smoking. Yvette got quickly down. They had suddenly come upon a disused quarry, cut into the slope of the road-side, and in this sudden lair, almost like a cave, were three caravans, dismantled for the winter. There was also deep at the back, a shelter built of boughs, as a stable for the horse. The grey, crude rock rose high above the caravans, and curved round towards the road. The floor was heaped chips of stone, with grasses growing among. It was a hidden, snug winter camp.

The elderly woman with the pack had gone in to one of the caravans, leaving the door open. Two children were peeping out, shewing black heads. The gipsy man gave a little call, as he backed his cart into the quarry, and an elderly man came out to help him untackle.

The gipsy himself went up the steps into the newest caravan, that had its door closed. Underneath, a tied-up dog ranged forth. It was a white hound spotted liver-coloured. It gave a low growl as Leo and Bob approached.

At the same moment, a dark-faced gipsy-woman with a pink shawl or kerchief round her head and big gold ear-rings in her ears, came down the steps of the newest caravan, swinging her flounced, voluminous green skirt. She was handsome in a bold, dark, long-faced way, just a bit wolfish. She looked like one of the bold, loping Spanish gipsies.

"Good-morning, my ladies and gentlemen," she said, eyeing the girls from her bold, predative eyes. She spoke with a certain foreign stiffness.

"Good afternoon!" said the girls.

"Which beautiful little lady like to hear her fortune? Give me her little hand?"

She was a tall woman, with a frightening way of reaching forward her neck like a menace. Her eyes went from face to face, very active, heartlessly searching out what she wanted. Meanwhile the man, apparently her husband, appeared at the top of the caravan steps smoking a pipe, and with a small, black-haired child in his arms. He stood on his limber legs, casually looking down on the group, as if from a distance, his long black lashes lifted from his full, conceited, impudent black eyes. There was something peculiarly transfusing in his stare. Yvette felt it, felt it in her knees. She pretended to be interested in the white-and-liver-coloured hound.

"How much do you want, if we all have our fortunes told?" asked Lottie Framley, as the six fresh-faced young Christians hung back rather reluctantly from this pagan pariah woman.

"All of you? ladies and gentlemen, all?" said the woman shrewdly.

"I don't want mine told! You go ahead!" cried Leo.

"Neither do I," said Bob. "You four girls."

"The four ladies?" said the gipsy woman, eyeing them shrewdly, after having looked at the boys. And she fixed her price. "Each one give me a sheeling, and a little bit more for luck? a little bit!" She smiled in a way that was more wolfish than cajoling, and the force of her will was felt, heavy as iron beneath the velvet of her words.

"All right," said Leo. "Make it a shilling a head. Don't spin it out too long."

"Oh, *you*!" cried Lucille at him. "We want to hear it *all."*

The woman took two wooden stools, from under a caravan, and placed them near the wheel. Then she took the tall, dark Lottie Framley by the hand, and bade her sit down. "You don't care if everybody hear?" she said, looking up curiously into Lottie's face.

Lottie blushed dark with nervousness, as the gipsy woman held her hand, and stroked her palm with hard, cruel-seeming fingers.

"Oh, I don't mind," she said.

The gipsy woman peered into the palm, tracing the lines of the hand with a hard, dark forefinger. But she seemed clean.

And slowly she told the fortune, while the others, standing listening, kept on crying out: "Oh, that's Jim Baggaley! Oh, I don't believe it! Oh, that's not true! A fair woman who lives beneath a tree! why whoever's that?" until Leo stopped them with a manly warning:

"Oh, hold on, girls! You give everything away."

Lottie retired blushing and confused, and it was Ella's turn. She was much more calm and shrewd, trying to read the oracular words. Lucille kept breaking out with: Oh, I say! The gipsy man at the top of the steps stood imperturbable, without any expression at all. But his bold eyes kept staring at Yvette, she could feel them on her cheek, on her neck, and she dared not look up. But Framley would sometimes look up at him, and got a level stare back, from the handsome face of the male gipsy, from the dark conceited proud eyes. It was a peculiar look, in the eyes that belonged to the tribe of the humble: the pride of the pariah, the half-sneering challenge of the outcast, who sneered at law-abiding men, and went on his own way. All the time, the gipsy man stood there, holding his child in his arms, looking on without being concerned.

Lucille was having her hand read,—"You have been across the sea, and there you met a man—a brown-haired man—but he was too old—"

"Oh, I *say!"* cried Lucille, looking round at Yvette.

But Yvette was abstracted, agitated, hardly heeding: in one of her mesmerised states.

"You will marry in a few years—not now, but a few years—perhaps four—and you will not be rich, but you will have plenty—enough—and you will go away, a long journey."

"With my husband, or without?" cried Lucille.

"With him—"

When it came to Yvette's turn, and the woman looked up boldly, cruelly, searching for a long time in her face, Yvette said nervously:

"I don't think I want mine told. No, I won't have mine told! No I won't, really!"

"You are afraid of some thing?" said the gipsy woman cruelly.

"No, it's not that—" Yvette fidgetted.

"You have some secret? You are afraid I shall say it. Come, would you like to go in the caravan, where nobody hears?"

The woman was curiously insinuating; while Yvette was always wayward, perverse. The look of perversity was on her soft, frail young face now, giving her a queer hardness.

"Yes!" she said suddenly. "Yes! I might do that!"

"Oh, I say!" cried the others. "Be a sport!"

"I don't think you'd *better!"* cried Lucille.

"Yes!" said Yvette, with that hard little way of hers. "I'll do that. I'll go in the caravan."

The gipsy woman called something to the man on the steps. He went into the caravan for a moment or two, then re-appeared, and came down the steps, setting the small child on its uncertain feet, and holding it by the hand. A dandy, in his polished black boots, tight black trousers and tight dark-green jersey, he walked slowly across, with the toddling child, to where the elderly gipsy was giving the roan horse a feed of oats, in the bough shelter between pits of grey rock, with dry bracken upon the stone-chip floor. He looked at Yvette as he passed, staring her full in the eyes, with his pariah's bold yet dishonest stare. Something hard inside her met his stare. But the surface of her body seemed to turn to water. Nevertheless, something hard in her registered the peculiar pure lines of his face, of his straight, pure nose, of his cheeks and temples. The curious dark, suave purity of all his body, outlined in the green jersey: a purity like a living sneer.

And as he loped slowly past her, on his flexible hips, it seemed to her still that he was stronger than she was. Of all the men she had ever seen, this one was the only one who was stronger than she was, in her own kind of strength, her own kind of understanding.

So, with curiosity, she followed the woman up the steps of the caravan, the skirts of her well-cut tan coat swinging and almost showing her knees, under the pale-green cloth dress. She had long, long-striding, fine legs, too slim rather than too thick, and she wore curiously-patterned pale-and-fawn stockings of fine wool, suggesting the legs of some delicate animal.

At the top of the steps she paused and turned, debonair, to the others, saying in her naïve, lordly way, so off-hand:

"I won't let her be long."

Her grey fur collar was open, showing her soft throat and pale green dress, her little, plaited tan-coloured hat came down to her ears, round her soft, fresh face. There was something soft and yet overbearing, unscrupulous, about her. She knew the gipsy man had turned to look at her. She was aware of the pure dark nape of his neck, the black hair groomed away. He watched as she entered his house.

What the gipsy told her, no one ever knew. It was a long time to wait, the others felt. Twilight was deepening on the gloom, and it was turning raw and cold. From the chimney of the second caravan came smoke and a smell of rich food. The horse was fed, a yellow blanket strapped round him, the two gipsy men talked together in the distance, in low tones. There was a peculiar feeling of silence and secrecy in that lonely, hidden quarry.

At last the caravan door opened, and Yvette emerged, bending forward and stepping with long, witch-like slim legs down the steps. There was a stooping, witch-like silence about her as she emerged on the twilight.

"Did it seem long?" she said vaguely, not looking at anybody and keeping her own counsel hard within her soft, vague waywardness. "I hope you weren't bored! Wouldn't tea be nice! Shall we go?"

"You get in!" said Bob. "I'll pay."

The gipsy-woman's full, metallic skirts of jade-green alpaca came swinging down the steps. She rose to her height, a big, triumphant-looking woman with a dark-wolf face. The pink cashmere kerchief, stamped with red roses, was slipping to one side over her black and crimped hair. She gazed at the young people in the twilight with bold arrogance.

Bob put two half-crowns in her hand.

"A little bit more, for luck, for your young lady's luck," she wheedled, like a wheedling wolf. "Another bit of silver, to bring you luck."

"You've got a shilling for luck, that's enough," said Bob calmly and quietly, as they moved away to the car.

"A little bit of silver! Just a little bit, for your luck in love!"

Yvette, with the sudden long, startling gestures of her long limbs, swung round as she was entering the car, and with long arm outstretched, strode and put something into the gipsy's hand, then stepped, bending her height, into the car.

"Prosperity to the beautiful young lady, and the gipsy's blessing on her," came the suggestive, half-sneering voice of the woman.

The engine *birred!* then *birred!* again more fiercely, and started. Leo switched on the lights, and immediately the quarry with the gipsies fell back into the blackness of night.

"Goodnight!" called Yvette's voice, as the car started. But hers was the only voice that piped up, chirpy and impudent in its nonchalance.

The headlights glared down the stone lane.

"Yvette, you've got to tell us what she said to you," cried Lucille, in the teeth of Yvette's silent will *not* to be asked.

"Oh, nothing at *all* thrilling," said Yvette, with false warmth. "Just the usual old thing: a dark man who means good luck, and a fair one who means bad: and a death in the family, which if it means Granny, won't be so *very* awful: and I shall marry when I'm twenty-three, and have heaps of money and heaps of love, and two children. All sounds very nice, but it's a bit too much of a good thing, you know."

"Oh, but why did you give her more money?"

"Oh well, I wanted to! You *have* to be a bit lordly with people like that—"

CHAPTER 4

There was a terrific rumpus down at the rectory, on account of Yvette and the Window Fund. After the war, Aunt Cissie had set her heart on a stained glass window in the church, as a memorial for the men of the parish who had fallen. But the bulk of the fallen had been non-conformists, so the memorial took the form of an ugly little monument in front of the Wesleyan chapel.

This did not vanquish Aunt Cissie. She canvassed, she had bazaars, she made the girls get up amateur theatrical shows, for her precious window. Yvette, who quite liked the acting and showing-off part of it, took charge of the farce called *Mary in the Mirror,* and gathered in the proceeds, which were to be paid to the Window Fund when accounts were settled. Each of the girls was supposed to have a money-box for the Fund.

Aunt Cissie, feeling that the united sums must now almost suffice, suddenly called in Yvette's box. It contained fifteen shillings. There was a moment of green horror.

"Where is all the rest?"

"Oh!" said Yvette, casually. "I just borrowed it. It wasn't so awfully much."

"What about the three pounds thirteen for *Mary in the Mirror?"* asked Aunt Cissie, as if the jaws of Hell were yawning.

"Oh quite! I just borrowed it. I can pay it back."

Poor Aunt Cissie! The green tumour of hate burst inside her, and there was a ghastly, abnormal scene, which left Yvette shivering with fear and nervous loathing.

Even the rector was rather severe.

"If you needed money, why didn't you tell me?" he said coldly. "Have you ever been refused anything in reason?"

"I—I thought it didn't matter," stammered Yvette.

"And what have you done with the money?"

"I suppose I've spent it," said Yvette, with wide, distraught eyes and a peaked face.

"Spent it, on what?"

"I can't remember everything: stockings and things, and I gave some of it away."

Poor Yvette! Her lordly airs and ways were already hitting back at her, on the reflex. The rector was angry: his face had a snarling, doggish look, a sort of sneer. He was afraid his daughter was developing some of the rank, tainted qualities of She-who-was-Cynthia.

"You *would* do the large with somebody else's money, wouldn't you?" he said, with a cold, mongrel sort of sneer, which showed what an utter unbeliever he was, at the heart. The inferiority of a heart which has no core of warm belief in it, no pride in life. He had utterly no belief in her.

Yvette went pale, and very distant. Her pride, that frail, precious flame which everybody tried to quench, recoiled like a flame blown far away, on a cold wind, as if blown out, and her face, white now and still like a snowdrop, the white snowflower of his conceit, seemed to have no life in it, only this pure, strange abstraction.

"He has no belief in me!" she thought in her soul. "I am really nothing to him. I am nothing, only a shameful thing. Everything is shameful, everything is shameful!"

A flame of passion or rage, while it might have overwhelmed or infuriated her, would not have degraded her as did her father's unbelief, his final attitude of a sneer against her.

He became a little afraid, in the silence of sterile thought. After all, he needed the *appearance* of love and belief and bright life, he would never dare to face the fat worm of his own unbelief, that stirred in his heart.

"What have you to say for yourself?" he asked.

She only looked at him from that senseless snowdrop face which haunted him with fear, and gave him a helpless sense of guilt. That other one, She-who-was-Cynthia, she had looked back at him with the same numb, white fear, the fear of his degrading unbelief, the worm which was his heart's core. He *knew* his heart's core was a fat, awful worm. His dread was lest anyone else should know. His anguish of hate was against anyone who knew, and recoiled.

He saw Yvette recoiling, and immediately his manner changed to the worldly old good-humoured cynic which he affected.

"Ah well!" he said. "You have to pay it back, my girl, that's all. I will advance you the money out of your allowance. But I shall charge you four per-cent a month interest. Even the devil himself must pay a percentage on his debts. Another time, if you can't trust yourself, don't handle money which isn't your own. Dishonesty isn't pretty."

Yvette remained crushed, and deflowered and humiliated. She crept about, trailing the rays of her pride. She had a revulsion even from herself. Oh, why had she ever touched the leprous money! Her whole flesh shrank as if it were defiled. Why was that? Why, why was that?

She admitted herself wrong in having spent the money. "Of course I shouldn't have done it. They are quite right to be angry," she said to herself.

But where did the horrible wincing of her flesh come from? Why did she feel she had caught some physical contagion?

"Where you're so *silly*, Yvette," Lucille lectured her: poor Lucille was in great distress—"is that you give yourself away to them all. You might *know* they'd find out. I could have raised the money for you, and saved all this bother. It's perfectly awful! But you never will think beforehand where your actions are going to land you! Fancy Aunt Cissie saying all those things to you! How *awful!* Whatever would Mamma have said, if she'd heard it?"

When things went very wrong, they thought of their mother, and despised their father and all the low brood of the Saywells. Their mother, of course, had belonged to a higher, if more dangerous and "immoral" world. More selfish, decidedly. But with a showier gesture. More unscrupulous and more easily moved to contempt: but not so humiliating. Yvette always considered that she got her fine, delicate flesh from her mother. The Saywells were all a bit leathery, and grubby somewhere inside. But then the Saywells never let you down.

Whereas the fine She-who-was-Cynthia had let the rector down with a bang, and his little children along with him. Her little children! They could not quite forgive her.

Only dimly, after the row, Yvette began to realise the other sanctity of herself, the sanctity of her sensitive, clean flesh and blood, which the Saywells with their so-called morality, succeeded in defiling. They always wanted to defile it. They were the life unbelievers. Whereas, perhaps She-who-was-Cynthia had only been a moral unbeliever.

Yvette went about dazed and peaked and confused. The rector paid in the money to Aunt Cissie, much to that lady's rage. The helpless tumour of her rage was still running. She would have liked to announce her niece's delinquency in the parish magazine. It was anguish to the destroyed woman that she could not publish the news to all the world. The selfishness! The selfishness! The selfishness!

Then the rector handed his daughter a little account with himself: her debt to him, interest thereon, the amount deducted from her small allowance. But to her credit he had placed a guinea, which was the fee he had to pay for complicity.

"As father of the culprit," he said humorously, "I am fined one guinea. And with that I wash the ashes out of my hair."

He was always generous about money. But somehow, he seemed to think that by being free about money he could absolutely call himself a generous man. Whereas he used money, even generosity, as a hold over her.

But he let the affair drop entirely. He was by this time more amused than anything, to judge from appearances. He thought still he was safe.

Aunt Cissie, however, could not get over her convulsion. One night when Yvette had gone rather early, miserably, to bed, when Lucille was away at a party, and she was lying with soft, peaked limbs aching with a sort of numbness and defilement, the door softly opened, and there stood Aunt Cissie, pushing her grey-green face through the opening of the door. Yvette started up in terror.

"Liar! Thief! Selfish little beast!" hissed the maniacal face of Aunt Cissie. "You little hypocrite! You liar! You selfish beast! You greedy little beast!"

There was such extraordinary impersonal hatred in that grey-green mask, and those frantic words, that Yvette opened her mouth to scream with hysterics. But Aunt Cissie shut the door as suddenly as she had opened it, and disappeared. Yvette leaped from her bed and turned the key. Then she crept back, half demented with fear of the squalid abnormal, half numbed with paralysis of damaged pride. And amid it all, up came a bubble of distracted laughter. It *was* so filthily ridiculous!

Aunt Cissie's behaviour did not hurt the girl so very much. It was after all somewhat fantastic. Yet hurt she was: in her limbs, in her body, in her sex, hurt. Hurt, numbed, and half destroyed, with only her nerves vibrating and jangled. And still so young, she could not conceive what was happening.

Only she lay and wished she were a gipsy. To live in a camp, in a caravan, and never set foot in a house, not know the existence of a parish, never look at a church. Her heart was hard with repugnance, against the rectory. She loathed these houses with their indoor sanitation and their bathrooms, and their extraordinary repulsiveness. She hated the rectory, and everything it implied. The whole stagnant, sewerage sort of life, where sewerage is never mentioned, but where it seems to smell from the centre of every two-legged inmate, from Granny to the servants, was foul. If gipsies had no bathrooms, at least they had no sewerage. There was fresh air. In the rectory there was *never* fresh air. And in the souls of the people, the air was stale till it stank.

Hate kindled her heart, as she lay with numbed limbs. And she thought of the words of the gipsy woman: "There is a dark man who never lived in a house. He loves you. The other people are treading on your heart. They will tread on your heart till you think it is dead. But the dark man will blow the one spark up into fire again, good fire. You will see what good fire."

Even as the woman was saying it, Yvette felt there was some duplicity somewhere. But she didn't mind. She hated with the cold, acrid hatred of a child the rectory interior, the sort of putridity in the life. She liked that big, swarthy, wolf-like gipsy-woman, with the big gold rings in her ears, the pink scarf over her wavy black hair, the tight bodice of brown velvet, the green, fan-like skirt. She liked her dusky, strong, relentless hands, that had pressed so firm, like wolf's paws, in Yvette's own soft palm. She liked her. She liked the danger and the covert fearlessness of her. She liked her covert, unyielding sex, that was immoral, but with a hard, defiant pride of its own. Nothing would ever get that woman under. She would despise the rectory and the rectory morality, utterly! She would strangle Granny with one hand. And she would have the same contempt for Daddy and for Uncle Fred, as men, as she would have for fat old slobbery Rover, the Newfoundland dog. A great, sardonic female contempt, for such domesticated dogs, calling themselves men.

And the gipsy man himself! Yvette quivered suddenly, as if she had seen his big, bold eyes upon her, with the naked insinuation of desire in them. The absolutely naked insinuation of desire made her life prone and powerless in the bed, as if a drug had cast her in a new molten mould.

She never confessed to anybody that two of the ill-starred Window Fund pounds had gone to the gipsy woman. What if Daddy and Aunt Cissie knew *that!* Yvette stirred luxuriously in the bed. The thought of the gipsy had released the life of her limbs, and crystallised in her heart the hate of the rectory: so that now she felt potent, instead of impotent.

When, later, Yvette told Lucille about Aunt Cissie's dramatic interlude in the bedroom doorway, Lucille was indignant.

"Oh, hang it all!" cried she. "She might let it drop now. I should think we've heard enough about it by now! Good heavens, you'd think Aunt Cissie was a perfect bird of paradise! Daddy's dropped it, and after all, it's his business if it's anybody's. Let Aunt Cissie shut up!"

It was the very fact that the rector had dropped it, and that he again treated the vague and inconsiderate Yvette as if she were some specially-licensed being, that kept Aunt Cissie's bile flowing. The fact that Yvette really was most of the time unaware of other people's feelings, and being unaware, couldn't care about them, nearly sent Aunt Cissie mad. Why should that young creature, with a delinquent mother, go through life as a privileged being, even unaware of other people's existence, though they were under her nose.

Lucille at this time was very irritable. She seemed as if she simply went a little unbalanced, when she entered the rectory. Poor Lucille, she was so thoughtful and responsible. She did all the extra troubling, thought about doctors, medicines, servants, and all that sort of thing. She slaved conscientiously at her job all day in town, working in a room with artificial light from ten till five. And she came home to have her nerves rubbed almost to a frenzy by Granny's horrible and persistent inquisitiveness and parasitic agedness.

The affair of the Window Fund had apparently blown over, but there remained a stuffy tension in the atmosphere. The weather continued bad. Lucille stayed at home on the afternoon of her half holiday, and did herself no good by it. The rector was in his study, she and Yvette were making a dress for the latter young woman, Granny was resting on the couch.

The dress was of blue silk velours, French material, and was going to be very becoming. Lucille made Yvette try it on again: she was nervously uneasy about the hang, under the arms.

"Oh bother!" cried Yvette, stretching her long, tender, childish arms, that tended to go bluish with the cold. "Don't be so frightfully *fussy,* Lucille! It's quite all right."

"If that's all the thanks I get, slaving my half day away making dresses for you, I might as well do something for myself!"

"Well, Lucille! You know I never *asked* you! You know you can't bear it unless you *do* supervise," said Yvette, with that irritating blandness of hers, as she raised her naked elbows and peered over her shoulder into the long mirror.

"Oh yes! you never *asked* me!" cried Lucille. "As if I didn't know what you meant, when you started sighing and flouncing about."

"I!" said Yvette, with vague surprise. "Why, when did I start sighing and flouncing about?"

"Of course you know you did."

"Did I? No, I didn't know! When was it?" Yvette could put a peculiar annoyance into her mild, straying questions.

"I shan't do another thing to this frock, if you don't stand still and *stop* it," said Lucille, in her rather sonorous, burning voice.

"You know you are most awfully nagging and irritable, Lucille," said Yvette, standing as if on hot bricks.

"Now Yvette!" cried Lucille, her eyes suddenly flashing in her sister's face, with wild flashes. "Stop it at once! Why should everybody put up with your abominable and overbearing temper!"

"Well, I don't know about *my* temper," said Yvette, writhing slowly out of the half-made frock, and slipping into her dress again.

Then, with an obstinate little look on her face, she sat down again at the table, in the gloomy afternoon, and began to sew at the blue stuff. The room was littered with blue clippings, the scissors were lying on the floor, the work-basket was spilled in chaos all over the table, and a second mirror was perched perilously on the piano.

Granny, who had been in a semi-coma, called a doze, roused herself on the big, soft couch and put her cap straight.

"I don't get much peace for my nap," she said, slowly feeling her thin white hair, to see that it was in order. She had heard vague noises.

Aunt Cissie came in, fumbling in a bag for a chocolate.

"I never saw such a mess!" she said. "You'd better clear some of that litter away, Yvette."

"All right," said Yvette. "I will in a minute."

"Which means never!" sneered Aunt Cissie, suddenly darting and picking up the scissors.

There was silence for a few moments, and Lucille slowly pushed her hands in her hair, as she read a book.

"You'd better clear away, Yvette," persisted Aunt Cissie.

"I will, before tea," replied Yvette, rising once more and pulling the blue dress over her head, flourishing her long, naked arms through the sleeveless armholes. Then she went between the mirrors, to look at herself once more.

As she did so, she sent the second mirror, that she had perched carelessly on the piano, sliding with a rattle to the floor. Luckily it did not break. But everybody started badly.

"She's smashed the mirror!" cried Aunt Cissie.

"Smashed a mirror! Which mirror! Who's smashed it?" came Granny's sharp voice.

"I haven't smashed anything," came the calm voice of Yvette. "It's quite all right."

"You'd better not perch it up there again," said Lucille.

Yvette, with a little impatient shrug at all the fuss, tried making the mirror stand in another place. She was not successful.

"If one had a fire in one's own room," she said crossly, "one needn't have a lot of people fussing when one wants to sew."

"Which mirror are you moving about?" asked Granny.

"One of our own, that came from the Vicarage," said Yvette rudely.

"Don't break it in *this* house, wherever it came from," said Granny.

There was a sort of family dislike for the furniture that had belonged to She-who-was-Cynthia. It was most of it shoved into the kitchen, and the servants' bedrooms.

"Oh, *I'm* not superstitious," said Yvette, "about mirrors or any of that sort of thing."

"Perhaps you're not," said Granny. "People who never take the responsibility for their own actions usually don't care what happens."

"After all," said Yvette, "I may say it's my own looking-glass, even if I did break it."

"And I say," said Granny, "that there shall be no mirrors broken in *this* house, if we can help it; no matter who they belong to, or did belong to. Cissie, have I got my cap straight?"

Aunt Cissie went over and straightened the old lady. Yvette loudly and irritatingly trilled a tuneless tune.

"And now, Yvette, will you please clear away," said Aunt Cissie.

"Oh bother!" cried Yvette angrily. "It's simply *awful* to live with a lot of people who are always nagging and fussing over trifles."

"What people, may I ask?" said Aunt Cissie ominously.

Another row was imminent. Lucille looked up with a queer cast in her eyes. In the two girls, the blood of She-who-was-Cynthia was roused.

"Of course you may ask! You know quite well I mean the people in this beastly house," said the outrageous Yvette.

"At least," said Granny, "we don't come of half-depraved stock."

There was a second's electric pause. Then Lucille sprang from her low seat, with sparks flying from her.

"You shut up!" she shouted, in a blast full upon the mottled majesty of the old lady.

The old woman's breast began to heave with heaven knows what emotions. The pause this time, as after the thunderbolt, was icy.

Then Aunt Cissie, livid, sprang upon Lucille, pushing her like a fury.

"Go to your room!" she cried hoarsely. "Go to your room!"

And she proceeded to push the white but fiery-eyed Lucille from the room. Lucille let herself be pushed, while Aunt Cissie vociferated:

"Stay in your room till you've apologised for this!—till you've apologised to the Mater for this!"

"I shan't apologise!" came the clear voice of Lucille, from the passage, while Aunt Cissie shoved her.

Aunt Cissie drove her more wildly upstairs.

Yvette stood tall and bemused in the sitting-room, with the air of offended dignity, at the same time bemused, which was so odd on her. She still was bare-armed, in the half-made blue dress. And even *she* was half-aghast at Lucille's attack on the majesty of age. But also, she was coldly indignant against Granny's aspersion of the maternal blood in their veins.

"Of course I meant no offense," said Granny.

"Didn't you!" said Yvette coolly.

"Of course not. I only said we're not depraved, just because we happen to be superstitious about breaking mirrors."

Yvette could hardly believe her ears. Had she heard right? Was it possible! Or was Granny, at her age, just telling a barefaced lie?

Yvette knew that the old woman was telling a cool, barefaced lie. But already, so quickly, Granny believed her own statement.

The rector appeared, having left time for a lull.

"What's wrong?" he asked cautiously, genially.

"Oh, nothing!" drawled Yvette. "Lucille told Granny to shut up, when she was saying something. And Aunt Cissie drove her up to her room. *Tant de bruit pour une omelette!* Though Lucille *was* a bit over the mark, that time."

The old lady couldn't quite catch what Yvette said.

"Lucille really will have to learn to control her nerves," said the old woman. "The mirror fell down, and it worried me. I said so to Yvette, and she said something about superstitions and the people in the beastly house. I told her the people in the house were not depraved, if they happened to mind when a mirror was broken. And at that Lucille flew at me and told me to shut up. It really is disgraceful how these children give way to their nerves. I know it's nothing but nerves."

Aunt Cissie had come in during this speech. At first even she was dumb. Then it seemed to her, it was as Granny had said.

"I have forbidden her to come down until she comes to apologise to the Mater," she said.

"I doubt if she'll apologise," said the calm, queenly Yvette, holding her bare arms.

"And I don't want any apology," said the old lady. "It is merely nerves. I don't know what they'll come to, if they have nerves like that, at their age! She must take Vibrofat.—I am sure Arthur would like his tea, Cissie!"

Yvette swept her sewing together, to go upstairs. And again she trilled her tune, rather shrill and tuneless. She was trembling inwardly.

"More glad rags!" said her father to her, genially.

"More glad rags!" she re-iterated sagely, as she sauntered upstairs, with her day dress over one arm. She wanted to console Lucille, and ask her how the blue stuff hung now.

At the first landing, she stood as she nearly always did, to gaze through the window that looked to the road and the bridge. Like the Lady of Shalott, she seemed always to imagine that someone would come along singing *Tirra-lirra!* or something equally intelligent, by the river.

CHAPTER 5

It was nearly tea-time. The snowdrops were out by the short drive going to the gate from the side of the house, and the gardener was pottering at the round, damp flower-beds, on the wet grass that sloped to the stream. Past the gate went the whitish muddy road, crossing the stone bridge almost immediately, and winding in a curve up to the steep, clustering, stony, smoking northern village, that perched over the grim stone mills which Yvette could see ahead down the narrow valley, their tall chimney long and erect.

The rectory was on one side the Papple, in the rather steep valley, the village was beyond and above, further down, on the other side the swift stream. At the back of the rectory the hill went up steep, with a grove of dark, bare larches, through which the road disappeared. And immediately across stream from the rectory, facing the house, the river-bank rose steep and bushy, up to the sloping, dreary meadows, that sloped up again to dark hillsides of trees, with grey rock cropping out.

But from the end of the house, Yvette could only see the road curving round past the wall with its laurel hedge, down to the bridge, then up again round the shoulder to that first hard cluster of houses in Papplewick village, beyond the dry-stone walls of the steep fields.

She always expected *something* to come down the slant of the road from Papplewick, and she always lingered at the landing window. Often a cart came, or a motor-car, or a lorry with stone, or a laborer, or one of the servants. But never anybody who sang *Tirra-lirra!* by the river. The tirra-lirraing days seemed to have gone by.

This day, however, round the corner on the white-grey road, between the grass and the low stone walls, a roan horse came stepping bravely and briskly down-hill, driven by a man in a cap, perched on the front of his light cart. The man swayed loosely to the swing of the cart, as the horse stepped down-hill, in the silent sombreness of the afternoon. At the back of the cart, long duster-brooms of reed and feather stuck out, nodding on their stalks of cane.

Yvette stood close to the window, and put the casement-cloth curtains behind her, clutching her bare upper arms with the hands.

At the foot of the slope the horse started into a brisk trot to the bridge. The cart rattled on the stone bridge, the brooms bobbed and flustered, the driver sat as if in a kind of dream, swinging along. It was like something seen in a sleep.

But as he crossed the end of the bridge, and was passing along the rectory wall, he looked up at the grim stone house that seemed to have backed away from the gate, under the hill. Yvette moved her hands quickly on her arms. And as quickly from under the peak of his cap, he had seen her, his swarthy predative face was alert.

He pulled up suddenly at the white gate, still gazing upwards at the landing window; while Yvette, always clasping her cold and mottled arms, still gazed abstractedly down at him, from the window.

His head gave a little, quick jerk of signal, and he led his horse well aside, on to the grass. Then, limber and alert, he turned back the tarpaulin of the cart, fetched out various articles, pulled forth two or three of the long brooms of reed or turkey-feathers, covered the cart, and turned towards the house, looking up at Yvette as he opened the white gate.

She nodded to him, and flew to the bathroom to put on her dress, hoping she had disguised her nod so that he wouldn't be sure she had nodded. Meanwhile she heard the hoarse deep roaring of that old fool, Rover, punctuated by the yapping of that young idiot, Trixie.

She and the housemaid arrived at the same moment at the sitting-room door.

"Was it the man selling brooms?" said Yvette to the maid. "All right!" and she opened the door. "Aunt Cissie, there's a man selling brooms. Shall I go?"

"What sort of a man?" said Aunt Cissie, who was sitting at tea with the rector and the Mater: the girls having been excluded for once from the meal.

"A man with a cart," said Yvette.

"A gipsy," said the maid.

Of course Aunt Cissie rose at once. She had to look at him.

The gipsy stood at the back door, under the steep dark bank where the larches grew. The long brooms flourished from one hand, and from the other hung various objects of shining copper and brass: a saucepan, a candlestick, plates of beaten copper. The man himself was neat and dapper, almost rakish, in his dark green cap and double-breasted green check coat. But his manner was subdued, very quiet: and at the same time proud, with a touch of condescension and aloofness.

"Anything today, lady?" he said, looking at Aunt Cissie with dark, shrewd, searching eyes, but putting a very quiet tenderness into his voice.

Aunt Cissie saw how handsome he was, saw the flexible curve of his lips under the line of black moustache, and she was fluttered. The merest hint of roughness or aggression on the man's part would have made her shut the door contemptuously in his face. But he managed to insinuate such a subtle suggestion of submission into his male bearing, that she began to hesitate.

"The candlestick is lovely!" said Yvette. "Did you make it?"

And she looked up at the man with her naïve, childlike eyes, that were as capable of double meanings as his own.

"Yes lady!" He looked back into her eyes for a second, with that naked suggestion of desire which acted on her like a spell, and robbed her of her will. Her tender face seemed to go into a sleep.

"It's awfully nice!" she murmured vaguely.

Aunt Cissie began to bargain for the candlestick: which was a low, thick stem of copper, rising from a double bowl. With patient aloofness the man attended to her, without ever looking at Yvette, who leaned against the doorway and watched in a muse.

"How is your wife?" she asked him suddenly, when Aunt Cissie had gone indoors to show the candlestick to the rector, and ask him if he thought it was worth it.

The man looked fully at Yvette, and a scarcely discernible smile curled his lips. His eyes did not smile: the insinuation in them only hardened to a glare.

"She's all right. When are you coming that way again?" he murmured, in a low, caressive, intimate voice.

"Oh, I don't know," said Yvette vaguely.

"You come Fridays, when I'm there," he said. Yvette gazed over his shoulder as if she had not heard him. Aunt Cissie returned, with the candlestick and the money to pay for it. Yvette turned nonchalant away, trilling one of her broken tunes, abandoning the whole affair with a certain rudeness.

Nevertheless, hiding this time at the landing window, she stood to watch the man go. What she wanted to know, was whether he really had any power over her. She did not intend him to see her this time.

She saw him go down to the gate, with his brooms and pans, and out to the cart. He carefully stowed away his pans and his brooms, and fixed down the tarpaulin over the cart. Then with a slow, effortless spring of his flexible loins, he was on the cart again, and touching the horse with the reins. The roan horse was away at once, the cart-wheels grinding uphill, and soon the man was gone, without looking round. Gone like a dream which was only a dream, yet which she could not shake off.

"No, he hasn't any power over me!" she said to herself: rather disappointed really, because she wanted somebody, or something to have power over her.

She went up to reason with the pale and overwrought Lucille, scolding her for getting into a state over nothing.

"What does it *matter,"* she expostulated, "if you told Granny to shut up! Why, everybody ought to be told to shut up, when they're being beastly. But she didn't mean it, you know. No, she didn't mean it. And she's quite sorry she said it. There's absolutely no reason to make a fuss. Come on, let's dress ourselves up and sail down to dinner like duchesses. Let's have our own back that way. Come on, Lucille!"

There was something strange and mazy, like having cobwebs over one's face, about Yvette's vague blitheness; her queer, misty side-stepping from an unpleasantness. It was cheering too. But it was like walking in one of those autumn mists, when gossamer strands blow over your face. You don't quite know where you are.

She succeeded, however, in persuading Lucille, and the girls got out their best party frocks: Lucille in green and silver, Yvette in a pale lilac colour with turquoise chenille threading. A little rouge and powder, and their best slippers, and the gardens of paradise began to blossom. Yvette hummed and looked at herself, and put on her most *dégagé* airs of one of the young marchionesses. She had an odd way of slanting her eyebrows and pursing her lips, and to all appearances detaching herself from every earthly consideration, and floating through the cloud of her own pearl-coloured reserves. It was amusing, and not quite convincing.

"Of course I am beautiful, Lucille," she said blandly. "And you're perfectly lovely, now you look a bit reproachful. Of course you're the most aristocratic of the two of us, with your nose! And now your eyes look reproachful, that adds an appealing look, and you're perfect, perfectly lovely. But I'm more *winning,* in a way.—Don't you agree?" She turned with arch, complicated simplicity to Lucille.

She was truly simple in what she said. It was just what she thought. But it gave no hint of the very different *feeling* that also preoccupied her: the feeling that she had been looked upon, not from the outside, but from the inside, from her secret female self. She was dressing herself up and looking her most dazzling, just to counteract the effect that the gipsy had had on her, when he had looked at her, and seen none of her pretty face and her pretty ways, but just the dark, tremulous, potent secret of her virginity.

The two girls started downstairs in state when the dinner-gong rang: but they waited till they heard the voice of the men. Then they sailed down and into the sitting-room, Yvette preening herself in her vague, debonair way, always a little bit absent; and Lucille shy, ready to burst into tears.

"My goodness gracious!" exclaimed Aunt Cissie, who was still wearing her dark-brown knitted sports coat. "What an apparition! Wherever do you think you're going?"

"We're dining with the family," said Yvette naïvely, "and we've put on our best gewgaws in honour of the occasion."

The rector laughed aloud, and Uncle Fred said:

"The family feels itself highly honoured."

Both the elderly men were quite gallant, which was what Yvette wanted.

"Come and let me feel your dresses, do!" said Granny. "Are they your best? It *is* a shame I can't see them."

"Tonight, Mater," said Uncle Fred, "we shall have to take the young ladies in to dinner, and live up to the honour. Will you go with Cissie?"

"I certainly will," said Granny. "Youth and beauty must come first."

"Well, tonight Mater!" said the rector, pleased.

And he offered his arm to Lucille, while Uncle Fred escorted Yvette.

But it was a draggled, dull meal, all the same. Lucille tried to be bright and sociable, and Yvette really was most amiable, in her vague, cobwebby way. Dimly, at the back of her mind, she was thinking: Why are we all only like mortal pieces of furniture? Why is nothing *important?*

That was her constant refrain, to herself: Why is nothing important? Whether she was in church, or at a party of young people, or dancing in the hotel in the city, the same little bubble of a question rose repeatedly on her consciousness: Why is nothing important?

There were plenty of young men to make love to her: even devotedly. But with impatience she had to shake them off. Why were they so unimportant?—so irritating!

She never even thought of the gipsy. He was a perfectly negligible incident. Yet the approach of Friday loomed strangely significant. "What are we doing on Friday?" she said to Lucille. To which Lucille replied that they were doing nothing. And Yvette was vexed.

Friday came, and in spite of herself she thought all day of the quarry off the road up high Bonsall Head. She wanted to be there. That was all she was conscious of. She wanted to be there. She had not even a dawning idea of going there. Besides, it was raining again. But as she sewed the blue dress, finishing it for the party up at Lambley Close, tomorrow, she just felt that her soul was up there, at the quarry, among the caravans, with the gipsies. Like one lost, or whose soul was stolen, she was not present in her body, the shell of her body. Her intrinsic body was away, at the quarry, among the caravans.

The next day, at the party, she had no idea that she was being sweet to Leo. She had no idea that she was snatching him away from the tortured Ella Framley. Not until, when she was eating her pistachio ice, he said to her:

"Why don't you and me get engaged, Yvette? I'm absolutely sure it's the right thing for us both."

Leo was a bit common, but good-natured, and well-off. Yvette quite liked him. But engaged! How perfectly silly! She felt like offering him a set of her silk underwear, to get engaged to.

"But I thought it was Ella!" she said, in wonder.

"Well! It might ha' been, but for you. It's your doings, you know! Ever since those gipsies told your fortune, I felt it was me or nobody, for you, and you or nobody, for me."

"Really!" said Yvette, simply lost in amazement. "Really!"

"Didn't you feel a bit the same?" he asked.

"Really!" Yvette kept on gasping softly, like a fish.

"You felt a bit the same, didn't you?" he said.

"What? About what?" she asked, coming to.

"About me, as I feel about you."

"Why? What? Getting engaged, you mean? I? no! Why how *could* I? I could never have dreamed of such an impossible thing."

She spoke with her usual heedless candour, utterly unoccupied with his feelings.

"What was to prevent you?" he said, a bit nettled. "I thought you did."

"Did you *really now?"* she breathed in amazement, with that soft, virgin, heedless candour which made her her admirers and her enemies.

She was so completely amazed, there was nothing for him to do but twiddle his thumbs in annoyance.

The music began, and he looked at her.

"No! I won't dance any more," she said, drawing herself up and gazing away rather loftily over the assembly, as if he did not exist. There was a touch of puzzled wonder on her brow, and her soft, dim virgin face did indeed suggest the snowdrop of her father's pathetic imagery.

"But of course *you* will dance," she said, turning to him with young condescension. "Do ask somebody to have this with you."

He rose, angry, and went down the room.

She remained soft and remote in her amazement. Expect Leo to propose to her! She might as well have expected old Rover the Newfoundland dog to propose to her. Get engaged, to any man on earth? No, good heavens, nothing more ridiculous could be imagined!

It was then, in a fleeting side-thought, that she realised that the gipsy existed. Instantly, she was indignant. Him, of all things! Him! Never!

"Now why?" she asked herself, again in hushed amazement. "Why? It's *absolutely* impossible: absolutely! So why is it?"

This was a nut to crack. She looked at the young men dancing, elbows out, hips prominent, waists elegantly in. They gave her no clue to her problem. Yet she did particularly dislike the forced elegance of the waists and the prominent hips, over which the well-tailored coats hung with such effeminate discretion.

"There is something about me which they don't see and never would see," she said angrily to herself. And at the same time, she was relieved that they didn't and couldn't. It made life so very much simpler.

And again, since she was one of the people who are conscious in visual images, she saw the dark-green jersey rolled on the black trousers of the gipsy, his fine, quick hips, alert as eyes. They were elegant. The elegance of these dancers seemed so stuffed, hips merely wadded with flesh. Leo the same, thinking himself such a fine dancer! and a fine figure of a fellow!

Then she saw the gipsy's face; the straight nose, the slender mobile lips, and the level, significant stare of the black eyes, which seemed to shoot her in some vital, undiscovered place, unerring.

She drew herself up angrily. How dared he look at her like that! So she gazed glaringly at the insipid beaux on the dancing floor. And she despised them. Just as the raggle-taggle gipsy women despise men who are not gipsies, despise their dog-like walk down the streets, she found herself despising this crowd. Where among them was the subtle, lonely, insinuating challenge that could reach her?

She did not want to mate with a house-dog.

Her sensitive nose turned up, her soft brown hair fell like a soft sheath round her tender, flowerlike face, as she sat musing. She seemed so virginal. At the same time, there was a touch of the tall young virgin *witch* about her, that made the house-dog men shy off. She might metamorphose into something uncanny before you knew where you were.

This made her lonely, in spite of all the courting. Perhaps the courting only made her lonelier.

Leo, who was a sort of mastiff among the house-dogs, returned after his dance, with fresh cheery-O! courage.

"You've had a little think about it, haven't you?" he said, sitting down beside her: a comfortable, well-nourished, determined sort of fellow. She did not know why it irritated her so unreasonably, when he hitched up his trousers at the knee, over his good-sized but not very distinguished legs, and lowered himself assuredly on to a chair.

"Have I?" she said vaguely. "About what?"

"You know what about," he said. "Did you make up your mind?"

"Make up my mind about what?" she asked, innocently.

In her upper consciousness, she truly had forgotten.

"Oh!" said Leo, settling his trousers again. "About me and you getting engaged, you know." He was almost as off-hand as she.

"Oh that's *absolutely* impossible," she said, with mild amiability, as if it were some stray question among the rest. "Why, I never even thought of it again. Oh, don't talk about that sort of nonsense! That sort of thing is *absolutely* impossible," she re-iterated like a child.

"That sort of thing is, is it?" he said, with an odd smile at her calm, distant assertion. "Well what sort of thing is possible, then? You don't want to die an old maid, do you?"

"Oh I don't mind," she said absently.

"I do," he said.

She turned round and looked at him in wonder.

"Why?" she said. "Why should you mind if I was an old maid?"

"Every reason in the world," he said, looking up at her with a bold, meaningful smile, that wanted to make its meaning blatant, if not patent.

But instead of penetrating into some deep, secret place, and shooting her there, Leo's bold and patent smile only hit her on the outside of the body, like a tennis ball, and caused the same kind of sudden irritated reaction.

"I think this sort of thing is awfully silly," she said, with minx-like spite. "Why, you're practically engaged to—to—" she pulled herself up in time—"probably half a dozen other girls. I'm not flattered by what you've said. I should hate it if anybody knew!—Hate it!—I shan't breathe a word of it, and I hope you'll have the sense not to.—There's Ella!"

And keeping her face averted from him, she sailed away like a tall, soft flower, to join poor Ella Framley.

Leo flapped his white gloves.

"Catty little bitch!" he said to himself. But he was of the mastiff type, he rather liked the kitten to fly in his face. He began definitely to single her out.

CHAPTER 6

The next week it poured again with rain. And this irritated Yvette with strange anger. She had intended it should be fine. Especially she insisted it should be fine towards the weekend. Why, she did not ask herself.

Thursday, the half-holiday, came with a hard frost, and sun. Leo arrived with his car, the usual bunch. Yvette disagreeably and unaccountably refused to go.

"No thanks, I don't feel like it," she said.

She rather enjoyed being Mary-Mary-quite-contrary.

Then she went for a walk by herself, up the frozen hills, to the Black Rocks.

The next day also came sunny and frosty. It was February, but in the north country the ground did not thaw in the sun. Yvette announced that she was going for a ride on her bicycle, and taking her lunch, as she might not be back till afternoon.

She set off, not hurrying. In spite of the frost, the sun had a touch of spring. In the park, the deer were standing in the distance, in the sunlight, to be warm. One doe, white spotted, walked slowly across the motionless landscape.

Cycling, Yvette found it difficult to keep her hands warm, even when bodily she was quite hot. Only when she had to walk up the long hill, to the top, and there was no wind.

The upland was very bare and clear, like another world. She had climbed on to another level. She cycled slowly, a little afraid of taking the wrong lane, in the vast maze of stone fences. As she passed along the lane she thought was the right one, she heard a faint tapping noise, with a slight metallic resonance.

The gipsy man was seated on the ground with his back to the cart-shaft, hammering a copper bowl. He was in the sun, bare-headed, but wearing his green jersey. Three small children were moving quietly round, playing in the horse's shelter: the horse and cart were gone. An old woman, bent, with a kerchief round her head, was cooking over a fire of sticks. The only sound was the rapid, ringing tap-tap-tap of the small hammer on the dull copper.

The man looked up at once, as Yvette stepped from her bicycle, but he did not move, though he ceased hammering. A delicate, barely discernible smile of triumph was on his face. The old woman looked round, keenly, from under her dirty grey hair. The man spoke a half-audible word to her, and she turned again to her fire. He looked up at Yvette.

"How are you all getting on?" she asked politely.

"All right, eh! You sit down a minute?" He turned as he sat, and pulled a stool from under the caravan for Yvette. Then, as she wheeled her bicycle to the side of the quarry, he started hammering again, with that bird-like, rapid light stroke.

Yvette went to the fire to warm her hands.

"Is this the dinner cooking?" she asked childishly, of the old gipsy, as she spread her long, tender hands, mottled red with the cold, to the embers.

"Dinner, yes!" said the old woman. "For him! And for the children."

She pointed with the long fork at the three black-eyed, staring children, who were staring at her from under their black fringes. But they were clean. Only the old woman was not clean. The quarry itself they had kept perfectly clean.

Yvette crouched in silence, warming her hands. The man rapidly hammered away with intervals of silence. The old hag slowly climbed the steps to the third, oldest caravan. The children began to play again, like little wild animals, quiet and busy.

"Are they your children?" asked Yvette, rising from the fire and turning to the man.

He looked her in the eyes, and nodded.

"But where's your wife?"

"She's gone out with the basket. They're all gone out, cart and all, selling things. I don't go selling things. I make them, but I don't go selling them. Not often. I don't often."

"You make all the copper and brass things?" she said.

He nodded, and again offered her the stool. She sat down.

"You said you'd be here on Fridays," she said. "So I came this way, as it was so fine."

"Very fine day!" said the gipsy, looking at her cheek, that was still a bit blanched by the cold, and the soft hair over her reddened ear, and the long, still mottled hands on her knee.

"You get cold, riding a bicycle?" he asked.

"My hands!" she said, clasping them nervously.

"You didn't wear gloves?"

"I did, but they weren't much good."

"Cold comes through," he said.

"Yes!" she replied.

The old woman came slowly, grotesquely down the steps of the caravan, with some enamel plates.

"The dinner cooked, eh?" he called softly.

The old woman muttered something, as she spread the plates near the fire. Two pots hung from a long iron horizontal-bar, over the embers of the fire. A little pan seethed on a small iron tripod. In the sunshine, heat and vapour wavered together.

He put down his tools and the pot, and rose from the ground.

"You eat something along of us?" he asked Yvette, not looking at her.

"Oh, I brought my lunch," said Yvette.

"You eat some stew?" he said. And again he called quietly, secretly to the old woman, who muttered in answer, as she slid the iron pot towards the end of the bar.

"Some beans, and some mutton in it," he said.

"Oh thanks awfully!" said Yvette. Then suddenly taking courage, added: "Well yes, just a very little, if I may."

She went across to untie her lunch from her bicycle, and he went up the steps to his own caravan. After a minute, he emerged, wiping his hands on a towel.

"You want to come up and wash your hands?" he said.

"No, I think not," she said. "They are clean."

He threw away his wash-water, and set off down the road with a high brass jug, to fetch clean water from the spring that trickled into a small pool, taking a cup to dip it with.

When he returned, he set the jug and the cup by the fire, and fetched himself a short log, to sit on. The children sat on the floor, by the fire, in a cluster, eating beans and bits of meat with spoon or fingers. The man on the log ate in silence, absorbedly. The woman made coffee in the black pot on the tripod, hobbling upstairs for the cups. There was silence in the camp. Yvette sat on her stool, having taken off her hat and shaken her hair in the sun.

"How many children have you?" Yvette asked suddenly.

"Say five," he replied slowly, as he looked up into her eyes.

And again the bird of her heart sank down and seemed to die. Vaguely, as in a dream, she received from him the cup of coffee. She was aware only of his silent figure, sitting like a shadow there on the log, with an enamel cup in his hand, drinking his coffee in silence. Her will had departed from her limbs, he had power over her: his shadow was on her.

And he, as he blew his hot coffee, was aware of one thing only, the mysterious fruit of her virginity, her perfect tenderness in the body.

At length he put down his coffee-cup by the fire, then looked round at her. Her hair fell across her face, as she tried to sip from the hot cup. On her face was that tender look of sleep, which a nodding flower has when it is full out, like a mysterious early flower, she was full out, like a snowdrop which spreads its three white wings in a flight into the waking sleep of its brief blossoming. The waking sleep of her full-opened virginity, entranced like a snowdrop in the sunshine, was upon her.

The gipsy, supremely aware of her, waited for her like the substance of shadow, as shadow waits and is there.

At length his voice said, without breaking the spell:

"You want to go in my caravan, now, and wash your hands?"

The childlike, sleep-waking eyes of her moment of perfect virginity looked into his, unseeing. She was only aware of the dark, strange effluence of him bathing her limbs, washing her at last purely will-less. She was aware of *him,* as a dark, complete power.

"I think I might," she said.

He rose silently, then turned to speak, in a low command, to the old woman. And then again he looked at Yvette, and putting his power over her, so that she had no burden of herself, or of action.

"Come!" he said.

She followed simply, followed the silent, secret, overpowering motion of his body in front of her. It cost her nothing. She was gone in his will.

He was at the top of the steps, and she at the foot, when she became aware of an intruding sound. She stood still, at the foot of the steps. A motor-car was coming. He stood at the top of the steps, looking round strangely. The old woman harshly called something, as with rapidly increasing sound, a car rushed near. It was passing.

Then they heard the cry of a woman's voice, and the brakes on the car. It had pulled up, just beyond the quarry.

The gipsy came down the steps, having closed the door of the caravan.

"You want to put your hat on," he said to her.

Obediently she went to the stool by the fire, and took up her hat. He sat down by the cart-wheel, darkly, and took up his tools. The rapid tap-tap-tap of his hammer, rapid and angry now like the sound of a tiny machine-gun, broke out just as the voice of the woman was heard crying:

"May we warm our hands at the camp fire?"

She advanced, dressed in a sleek but bulky coat of sable fur. A man followed, in a blue great-coat; pulling off his fur gloves and pulling out a pipe.

"It looked so tempting," said the woman in the coat of many dead little animals, smiling a broad, half-condescending, half-hesitant simper, around the company.

No one said a word.

She advanced to the fire, shuddering a little inside her coat, with the cold. They had been driving in an open car.

She was a very small woman, with a rather large nose: probably a Jewess. Tiny almost as a child, in that sable coat she looked much more bulky than she should, and her wide, rather resentful brown eyes of a spoilt Jewess gazed oddly out of her expensive get-up.

She crouched over the low fire, spreading her little hands, on which diamonds and emeralds glittered.

"Ugh!" she shuddered. "Of course we ought not to have come in an open car! But my husband won't even let me say I'm cold!" She looked round at him with her large, childish, reproachful eyes, that had still the canny shrewdness of a bourgeois Jewess: a rich one, probably.

Apparently she was in love, in a Jewess's curious way, with the big, blond man. He looked back at her with his abstracted blue eyes, that seemed to have no lashes, and a small smile creased his smooth, curiously naked cheeks. The smile didn't mean anything at all.

He was a man one connects instantly with winter sports, skiing and skating. Athletic, unconnected with life, he slowly filled his pipe, pressing in the tobacco with long, powerful reddened finger.

The Jewess looked at him to see if she got any response from him. Nothing at all, but that odd, blank smile. She turned again to the fire, tilting her eyebrows and looking at her small, white, spread hands.

He slipped off his heavily lined coat, and appeared in one of the handsome, sharp-patterned knitted jerseys, in yellow and grey and black, over well-cut trousers, rather wide. Yes, they were both expensive! And he had a magnificent figure, an athletic, prominent chest. Like an experienced camper, he began building the fire together, quietly: like a soldier on campaign.

"D'you think they'd mind if we put some fir-cones on, to make a blaze?" he asked of Yvette, with a silent glance at the hammering gipsy.

"Love it, I should think," said Yvette, in a daze, as the spell of the gipsy slowly left her, feeling stranded and blank.

The man went to the car, and returned with a little sack of cones, from which he drew a handful.

"Mind if we make a blaze?" he called to the gipsy.

"Eh?"

"Mind if we make a blaze with a few cones?"

"You go ahead!" said the gipsy.

The man began placing the cones lightly, carefully on the red embers. And soon, one by one, they caught fire, and burned like roses of flame, with a sweet scent.

"Ah lovely! lovely!" cried the little Jewess, looking up at her man again. He looked down at her quite kindly, like the sun on ice. "Don't you love fire! Oh, I love it!" the little Jewess cried to Yvette, across the hammering.

The hammering annoyed her. She looked round with a slight frown on her fine little brows, as if she would bid the man stop. Yvette looked round too. The gipsy was bent over his copper bowl, legs apart, head down, lithe arm lifted. Already he seemed so far from her.

The man who accompanied the little Jewess strolled over to the gipsy, and stood in silence looking down on him, holding his pipe to his mouth. Now they were two men, like two strange male dogs, having to sniff one another.

"We're on our honeymoon," said the little Jewess, with an arch, resentful look at Yvette. She spoke in a rather high, defiant voice, like some bird, a jay, or a crook, calling.

"Are you really?" said Yvette.

"Yes! Before we're married! Have you heard of Simon Fawcett?"—she named a wealthy and well-known engineer of the north country. "Well, I'm Mrs. Fawcett, and he's just divorcing me!" She looked at Yvette with curious defiance and wistfulness.

"Are you really!" said Yvette.

She understood now the look of resentment and defiance in the little Jewess' big, childlike brown eyes. She was an honest little thing, but perhaps her honesty was *too* rational. Perhaps it partly explained the notorious unscrupulousness of the well-known Simon Fawcett.

"Yes! As soon as we get the divorce, I'm going to marry Major Eastwood."

Her cards were now all on the table. She was not going to deceive anybody.

Behind her, the two men were talking briefly. She glanced round, and fixed the gipsy with her big brown eyes.

He was looking up, as if shyly, at the big fellow in the sparkling jersey, who was standing pipe in mouth, man to man, looking down.

"With the horses back of Arras," said the gipsy, in a low voice.

They were talking war. The gipsy had served with the artillery teams, in the Major's own regiment.

"Ein schöner Mensch!" said the Jewess. "A handsome man, eh?"

For her, too, the gipsy was one of the common men, the Tommies.

"Quite handsome!" said Yvette.

"You are cycling?" asked the Jewess in a tone of surprise.

"Yes! Down to Papplewick. My father is rector of Papplewick: Mr. Saywell!"

"Oh!" said the Jewess. "I know! A clever writer! Very clever! I have read him."

The fir-cones were all consumed already, the fire was a tall pile now of crumbling, shattering fire-roses. The sky was clouding over for afternoon. Perhaps towards evening it would snow.

The Major came back, and slung himself into his coat.

"I thought I remembered his face," he said. "One of our grooms, A. 1. man with horses."

"Look!" cried the Jewess to Yvette. "Why don't you let us motor you down to Normanton. We live in Scoresby. We can tie the bicycle on behind."

"I think I will, "said Yvette.

"Come!" called the Jewess to the peeping children, as the blond man wheeled away the bicycle. "Come! Come here!" and taking out her little purse, she held out a shilling.

"Come!" she cried. "Come and take it!"

The gipsy had laid down his work, and gone into his caravan. The old woman called hoarsely to the children, from the enclosure. The two elder children came stealing forward. The Jewess gave them the two bits of silver, a shilling and a florin, which she had in her purse, and again the hoarse voice of the unseen old woman was heard.

The gipsy descended from his caravan and strolled to the fire. The Jewess searched his face with the peculiar bourgeois boldness of her race.

"You were in the war, in Major Eastwood's regiment!" she said.

"Yes, lady!"

"Imagine you both being here now!—It's going to snow—" she looked up at the sky.

"Later on," said the man, looking at the sky.

He too had gone inaccessible. His race was very old, in its peculiar battle with established society, and had no conception of winning. Only now and then it could score.

But since the war, even the old sporting chance of scoring now and then, was pretty well quenched. There was no question of yielding. The gipsy's eyes still had their bold look: but it was hardened and directed far away, the touch of insolent intimacy was gone. He had been through the war.

He looked at Yvette.

"You're going back in the motor-car?" he said.

"Yes!" she replied, with a rather mincing mannerism. "The weather is so treacherous!"

"Treacherous weather!" he repeated, looking at the sky.

She could not tell in the least what his feelings were. In truth, she wasn't very much interested. She was rather fascinated, now, by the little Jewess, mother of two children, who was taking her wealth away from the well-known engineer and transferring it to the penniless, sporting young Major Eastwood, who must be five or six years younger than she. Rather intriguing!

The blond man returned.

"A cigarette, Charles!" cried the little Jewess, plaintively.

He took out his case, slowly, with his slow, athletic movement. Something sensitive in him made him slow, cautious, as if he had hurt himself against people. He gave a cigarette to his wife, then one to Yvette, then offered the case, quite simply, to the gipsy. The gipsy took one.

"Thank you sir!"

And he went quietly to the fire, and stooping, lit it at the red embers. Both women watched him.

"Well goodbye!" said the Jewess, with her odd bourgeois free-masonry. "Thank you for the warm fire."

"Fire is everybody's," said the gipsy.

The young child came toddling to him.

"Goodbye!" said Yvette. "I hope it won't snow for you."

"We don't mind a bit of snow," said the gipsy.

"Don't you?" said Yvette. "I should have thought you would!"

"No!" said the gipsy.

She flung her scarf royally over her shoulder, and followed the fur coat of the Jewess, which seemed to walk on little legs of its own.

CHAPTER 7

Yvette was rather thrilled by the Eastwoods, as she called them. The little Jewess had only to wait three months now, for the final decree. She had boldly rented a small summer cottage, by the moors up at Scoresby, not far from the hills. Now it was dead winter, and she and the Major lived in comparative isolation, without any maid-servant. He had already resigned his commission in the regular army, and called himself Mr. Eastwood. In fact, they were already Mr. and Mrs. Eastwood, to the common world.

The little Jewess was thirty-six, and her two children were both over twelve years of age. The husband had agreed that she should have the custody, as soon as she was married to Eastwood.

So there they were, this queer couple, the tiny, finely-formed little Jewess with her big, resentful, reproachful eyes, and her mop of carefully-barbered black, curly hair, an elegant little thing in her way, and the big, pale-eyed young man, powerful and wintry, the remnant surely of some old uncanny Danish stock: living together in a small modern house near the moors and the hills, and doing their own housework.

It was a funny household. The cottage was hired furnished, but the little Jewess had brought along her dearest pieces of furniture. She had an odd little taste for the rococco, strange curving cupboards inlaid with mother of pearl, tortoiseshell, ebony, heaven knows what; strange tall flamboyant chairs, from Italy, with sea-green brocade: astonishing saints with wind-blown, richly-coloured carven garments and pink faces: shelves of weird old Saxe and Capo di Monte figurines: and finally, a strange assortment of astonishing pictures painted on the back of glass, done, probably in the early years of the nineteenth century, or in the late eighteenth.

In this crowded and extraordinary interior she received Yvette, when the latter made a stolen visit. A whole system of stoves had been installed into the cottage, every corner was warm, almost hot. And there was the tiny rococco figurine of the Jewess herself, in a perfect little frock, and an apron, putting slices of ham on the dish, while the great snow-bird of a major, in a white sweater and grey trousers, cut bread, mixed mustard, prepared coffee, and did all the rest. He had even made the dish of jugged hare which followed the cold meats and caviare.

The silver and the china were really valuable, part of the bride's trousseau. The Major drank beer from a silver mug, the little Jewess and Yvette had champagne in lovely glasses, the Major brought in coffee. They talked away. The little Jewess had a burning indignation against her first husband. She was intensely moral, so moral, that she was a divorcée. The Major too, strange wintry bird, so powerful, handsome, too, in his way, but pale round the eyes as if he had no eyelashes, like a bird, he too had a curious indignation against life, because of the false morality. That powerful, athletic chest hid a strange, snowy sort of anger. And his tenderness for the little Jewess was based on his sense of outraged justice, the abstract morality of the north blowing him, like a strange wind, into isolation.

As the afternoon drew on, they went to the kitchen, the Major pushed back his sleeves, showing his powerful athletic white arms, and carefully, deftly washed the dishes, while the woman wiped. It was not for nothing his muscles were trained. Then he went round attending to the stoves of the small house, which only needed a moment or two of care each day. And after this, he brought out the small, closed car and drove Yvette home, in the rain, depositing her at the back gate, a little wicket among the larches, through which the earthen steps sloped downwards to the house.

She was really amazed by this couple.

"Really, Lucille!" she said. "I do meet the most extraordinary people!" And she gave a detailed description.

"I think they sound rather nice!" said Lucille. "I like the Major doing the housework, and looking so frightfully Bond-streety with it all. I should think, *when they're married,* it would be rather fun knowing them."

"Yes!" said Yvette vaguely. "Yes! Yes, it would!"

The very strangeness of the connection between the tiny Jewess and that pale-eyed, athletic young officer made her think again of her gipsy, who had been utterly absent from her consciousness, but who now returned with sudden painful force.

"What is it, Lucille," she asked, "that brings people together? People like the Eastwoods, for instance? and Daddy and Mamma, so frightfully unsuitable?—and that gipsy woman who told my fortune, like a great horse, and the gipsy man, so fine and delicately cut? What is it?"

"I suppose it's sex, whatever that is," said Lucille.

"Yes, what is it? It's not really anything *common,* like common sensuality, you know, Lucille. It really isn't!"

"No, I suppose not," said Lucille. "Anyhow I suppose it needn't be."

"Because you see, the *common* fellows, you know, who make a girl feel *low:* nobody cares much about them. Nobody feels any connection with them. Yet they're supposed to be the sexual sort."

"I suppose," said Lucille, "there's the low sort of sex, and there's the other sort, that isn't low. It's frightfully complicated, really! I *loathe* common fellows. And I never feel anything *sexual*—" she laid a rather disgusted stress on the word—"for fellows who aren't common. Perhaps I haven't got any sex."

"That's just it!" said Yvette. "Perhaps neither of us has. Perhaps we haven't really *got* any sex, to connect us with men."

"How horrible it sounds: *connect us with men*!" cried Lucille, with revulsion. "Wouldn't you hate to be connected with men that way? Oh I think it's an awful pity there has to *be* sex! It would be so much better if we could still be men and women, without that sort of thing."

Yvette pondered. Far in the background was the image of the gipsy as he had looked round at her, when she had said: The weather is so treacherous. She felt rather like Peter when the cock crew, as she denied him. Or rather, she did not deny the gipsy; she didn't care about his part in the show, anyhow. It was some hidden part of herself which she denied: that part which mysteriously and unconfessedly responded to him. And it was a strange, lustrous black cock which crew in mockery of her.

"Yes!" she said vaguely. "Yes! Sex is an awful bore, you know Lucille. When you haven't got it, you feel you *ought* to have it, somehow. And when you've got it—or *if* you have it—" she lifted her head and wrinkled her nose disdainfully—"you hate it."

"Oh I don't know!" cried Lucille. "I think I should *like* to be awfully in love with a man."

"You think so!" said Yvette, again wrinkling her nose. "But if you were you wouldn't."

"How do you know?" asked Lucille.

"Well, I don't really," said Yvette. "But I think so! Yes, I think so!"

"Oh, it's very likely!" said Lucille disgustedly. "And anyhow one would be sure to get out of love again, and it would be merely disgusting."

"Yes," said Yvette. "It's a problem." She hummed a little tune.

"Oh hang it all, it's not a problem for us two, yet. We're neither of us really in love, and we probably never shall be, so the problem is settled that way."

"I'm not so sure!" said Yvette sagely. "I'm not so sure. I believe, one day, I shall fall *awfully* in love."

"Probably you never will," said Lucille brutally. "That's what most old maids are thinking all the time."

Yvette looked at her sister from pensive but apparently insouciant eyes.

"Is it?" she said. "Do you really think so, Lucille? How perfectly awful for them, poor things! Why ever do they *care?"*

"Why do they?" said Lucille. "Perhaps they don't, really.—Probably it's all because people say: *Poor old girl, she couldn't catch a man."*

"I suppose it is!" said Yvette. "They get to mind the beastly things people always do say about old maids. What a shame!"

"Anyhow we have a good time, and we do have lots of boys who make a fuss of us," said Lucille.

"Yes!" said Yvette. "Yes! But I couldn't possibly marry any of them."

"Neither could I," said Lucille. "But why shouldn't we! Why should we bother about marrying, when we have a perfectly good time with the boys who are awfully good sorts, and you must say, Yvette, awfully sporting and *decent* to us."

"Oh, they are!" said Yvette absently.

"I think it's time to think of marrying somebody," said Lucille, "when you feel you're *not* having a good time any more. Then marry, and just settle down."

"Quite!" said Yvette.

But now, under all her bland, soft amiability, she was annoyed with Lucille. Suddenly she wanted to turn her back on Lucille.

Besides, look at the shadows under poor Lucille's eyes, and the wistfulness in the beautiful eyes themselves. Oh, if some awfully nice, kind, protective sort of man would but marry her! And if the sporting Lucille would let him!

Yvette did not tell the rector, nor Granny, about the Eastwoods. It would only have started a lot of talk which she detested. The rector wouldn't have minded, for himself, privately. But he too knew the necessity of keeping as clear as possible from that poisonous, many-headed serpent, the tongue of the people.

"But I don't *want* you to come if your father doesn't know," cried the little Jewess.

"I suppose I'll have to tell him," said Yvette. "I'm sure he doesn't mind, really. But if he knew, he'd have to, I suppose."

The young officer looked at her with an odd amusement, bird-like and unemotional, in his keen eyes. He too was by way of falling in love with Yvette. It was her peculiar virgin tenderness, and her straying, absent-minded detachment from things, which attracted him.

She was aware of what was happening, and she rather preened herself. Eastwood piqued her fancy. Such a smart young officer, awfully good class, so calm and amazing with a motor-car, and quite a champion swimmer, it was intriguing to see him quietly, calmly washing dishes, smoking his pipe, doing his job so alert and skilful. Or, with the same interested care with which he made his investigation into the mysterious inside of an automobile, concocting jugged hare in the cottage kitchen. Then going out in the icy weather and cleaning his car till it looked like a live thing, like a cat when she has licked herself. Then coming in to talk so unassumingly and responsively, if briefly, with the little Jewess. And apparently, never bored. Sitting at the window with his pipe, in bad weather, silent for hours, abstracted, musing, yet with his athletic body alert in its stillness.

Yvette did not flirt with him. But she *did* like him.

"But what about your future?" she asked him.

"What about it?" he said, taking his pipe from his mouth, the unemotional point of a smile in his bird's eyes.

"A career! Doesn't every man have to carve out a career?—like some huge goose with gravy?" She gazed with odd naïveté into his eyes.

"I'm perfectly all right today, and I shall be all right tomorrow," he said, with a cold, decided look. "Why shouldn't my future be continuous todays and tomorrows?"

He looked at her with unmoved searching.

"Quite!" she said. "I hate jobs, and all that side of life." But she was thinking of the Jewess's money.

To which he did not answer. His anger was of the soft, snowy sort, which comfortably muffles the soul.

They had come to the point of talking philosophically together. The little Jewess looked a bit wan. She was curiously naïve and not possessive, in her attitude to the man. Nor was she at all catty with Yvette. Only rather wan, and dumb.

Yvette, on a sudden impulse, thought she had better clear herself.

"I think life's *awfully* difficult," she said.

"Life is!" cried the Jewess.

"What's so beastly, is that one is supposed to *fall in love,* and get married!" said Yvette, curling up her nose.

"Don't you *want* to fall in love and get married?" cried the Jewess, with great glaring eyes of astounded reproach.

"No, not particularly!" said Yvette. "Especially as one feels there's nothing else to do. It's an awful chickencoop one has to run into."

"But you don't know what love is?" cried the Jewess.

"No!" said Yvette. "Do you?"

"I!" bawled the tiny Jewess. "I! My goodness, don't I!" She looked with reflective gloom at Eastwood, who was smoking his pipe, the dimples of his disconnected amusement showing on his smooth, scrupulous face. He had a very fine, smooth skin, which yet did not suffer from the weather, so that his face looked naked as a baby's. But it was not a round face: it was characteristic enough, and took queer ironical dimples, like a mask which is comic but frozen.

"Do you mean to say you don't know what love is?" insisted the Jewess.

"No!" said Yvette, with insouciant candour. "I don't believe I do! Is it awful of me, at my age?"

"Is there never any man that makes you feel quite, quite different?" said the Jewess, with another big-eyed look at Eastwood. He smoked, utterly unimplicated.

"I don't think there is," said Yvette. "Unless—yes!—unless it is that gipsy"—she had put her head pensively sideways.

"Which gipsy?" bawled the little Jewess.

"The one who was a Tommy and looked after horses in Major Eastwood's regiment in the war," said Yvette coolly.

The little Jewess gazed at Yvette with great eyes of stupor.

"You're not in love with that *gipsy!"* she said.

"Well!" said Yvette. "I don't know. He's the only one that makes me feel—different! He really is!"

"But how? How? Has he ever *said* anything to you?"

"No! No!"

"Then how? What has he done?"

"Oh, just looked at me!"

"How?"

"Well you see, I don't know. But different! Yes, different! Different, quite different from the way any man ever looked at me."

"But *how* did he look at you?" insisted the Jewess.

"Why—as if he really, but *really, desired* me," said Yvette, her meditative face looking like the bud of a flower.

"What a vile fellow! What *right* had he to look at you like that?" cried the indignant Jewess.

"A cat may look at a king," calmly interposed the Major, and now his face had the smiles of a cat's face.

"You think he oughtn't to?" asked Yvette, turning to him.

"Certainly not! A gipsy fellow, with half a dozen dirty women trailing after him! Certainly not!" cried the tiny Jewess.

"I wondered!" said Yvette. "Because it *was* rather wonderful, really! And it *was* something quite different in my life."

"I think," said the Major, taking his pipe from his mouth, "that desire is the most wonderful thing in life. Anybody who can really feel it, is a king, and I envy nobody else!" He put back his pipe.

The Jewess looked at him stupefied.

"But Charles!" she cried. "Every common low man in Halifax feels nothing else!"

He again took his pipe from his mouth.

"That's merely appetite," he said.

And he put back his pipe.

"You think the gipsy is a real thing?" Yvette asked him. He lifted his shoulders.

"It's not for me to say," he replied. "If I were you, I should know, I shouldn't be asking other people."

"Yes—but—" Yvette trailed out.

"Charles! You're wrong! How *could* it be a real thing! As if she could possibly marry him and go round in a caravan!"

"I didn't say marry him," said Charles.

"Or a love affair! Why it's monstrous! What would she think of herself!—That's not love! That's—that's prostitution!"

Charles smoked for some moments.

"That gipsy was the best man we had, with horses. Nearly died of pneumonia. I thought he *was* dead. He's a resurrected man to me. I'm a resurrected man myself, as far as that goes." He looked at Yvette. "I was buried for twenty hours under snow," he said. "And not much the worse for it, when they dug me out."

There was a frozen pause in the conversation.

"Life's awful!" said Yvette.

"They dug me out by accident," he said.

"Oh!—" Yvette trailed slowly. "It might be destiny, you know."

To which he did not answer.

Chapter 8

The rector heard about Yvette's intimacy with the Eastwoods, and she was somewhat startled by the result. She had thought he wouldn't care. Verbally, in his would-be humorous fashion, he was so entirely unconventional, such a frightfully good sport. As he said himself, he was a conservative anarchist, which meant, he was like a great many more people, a mere unbeliever. The anarchy extended to his humorous talk, and his secret thinking. The conservatism based on a mongrel fear of the anarchy, controlled every action. His thoughts, secretly, were something to be scared of. Therefore, in his life, he was fanatically afraid of the unconventional.

When his conservatism and his abject sort of fear were uppermost, he always lifted his lip and bared his teeth a little, in a dog-like sneer.

"I hear your latest friends are the half-divorced Mrs. Fawcett and the *maquereau* Eastwood," he said to Yvette.

She didn't know what a *maquereau* was, but she felt the poison in the rector's fangs.

"I just know them," she said. "They're awfully nice, really. And they'll be married in about a month's time."

The rector looked at her insouciant face with hatred. Somewhere inside him, he was cowed, he had been born cowed. And those who are born cowed are natural slaves, and deep instinct makes them fear with prisonous fear those who might suddenly snap the slave's collar round their necks.

It was for this reason the rector had so abjectly curled up, who still so abject curled up before She-who-was-Cynthia: because of his slave's fear of her contempt, the contempt of a born-free nature for a base-born nature.

Yvette too had a free-born quality. She too, one day, would know him, and clap the slave's collar of her contempt round his neck.

But should she? He would fight to the death, this time, first. The slave in him was cornered this time, like a cornered rat, and with the courage of a cornered rat.

"I suppose they're your sort!" he sneered.

"Well they are, really," she said, with that blithe vagueness. "I do like them awfully. They seem so solid, you know, so honest."

"You've got a peculiar notion of honesty!" he sneered. "A young sponge going off with a woman older than himself, so that he can live on her money! The woman leaving her home and her children! I don't know where you get your idea of honesty. Not from me, I hope. —And you seem to be very well acquainted with them, considering you say you just know them. Where did you meet them?"

"When I was out bicycling. They came along in their car, and we happened to talk. She told me at once who she was, so that I shouldn't make a mistake. She is honest."

Poor Yvette was struggling to bear up.

"And how often have you seen them since?"

"Oh, I've just been over twice."

"Over where?"

"To their cottage in Scoresby."

He looked at her in hate, as if he could kill her. And he backed away from her, against the window-curtains of his study, like a rat at bay. Somewhere in his mind he was thinking unspeakable depravities about his daughter, as he had thought them of She-who-was-Cynthia. He was powerless against the lowest insinuations of his own mind. And these depravities which he attributed to the still-uncowed, but frightened girl in front of him, made him recoil, showing all his fangs in his handsome face.

"So you just know them, do you?" he said. "Lying is in your blood, I see. I don't believe you get it from me."

Yvette half averted her mute face, and thought of Granny's barefaced prevarication. She did not answer.

"What takes you creeping round such couples?" he sneered. "Aren't there enough decent people in the world, for you to know? Anyone would think you were a stray dog, having to run round indecent couples, because the decent ones wouldn't have you. Have you got something worse than lying, in your blood?"

"What have I got, worse than lying in my blood?" she asked. A cold deadness was coming over her. Was she abnormal, one of the semicriminal abnormals? It made her feel cold and dead.

In his eyes, she was just brazening out the depravity that underlay her virgin, tender, bird-like face. She-who-was-Cynthia had been like this: a snowflower. And he had convulsions of sadistic horror, thinking what might be the *actual* depravity of She-who-was-Cynthia. Even his *own* love for her, which had been the lust love of the born cowed, had been a depravity, in secret, to him. So what must an illegal love be?

"You know best yourself, what you have got," he sneered. "But it is something you had best curb, and quickly, if you don't intend to finish in a criminal-lunacy asylum."

"Why?" she said, pale and muted, numbed with frozen fear. "Why criminal lunacy? What have I done?"

"That is between you and your Maker," he jeered. "I shall never ask. But certain tendencies end in criminal lunacy, unless they are curbed in time."

"Do you mean like knowing the Eastwoods?" asked Yvette, after a pause of numb fear.

"Do I mean like nosing round such people as Mrs. Fawcett, a Jewess, and ex-Major Eastwood, a man who goes off with an older woman for the sake of her money? Why yes, I do!"

"But you *can't* say that," cried Yvette. "He's an awfully simple, straightforward man."

"He is apparently one of your sort."

"Well.—In a way, I thought he was. I thought you'd like him too," she said, simply, hardly knowing what she said.

The rector backed into the curtains, as if the girl menaced him with something fearful.

"Don't say any more," he snarled, abject. "Don't say any more. You've said too much, to implicate you. I don't want to learn any more horrors."

"But what horrors?" she persisted.

The very naïveté of her unscrupulous innocence repelled him, cowed him still more.

"Say no more!" he said, in a low, hissing voice. "But I will kill you before you shall go the way of your mother."

She looked at him, as he stood there backed against the velvet curtains of his study, his face yellow, his eyes distraught like a rat's with fear and rage and hate, and a numb, frozen loneliness came over her. For her too, the meaning had gone out of everything.

It was hard to break the frozen, sterile silence that ensued. At last, however, she looked at him. And in spite of herself, beyond her own knowledge, the contempt for him was in her young, clear, baffled eyes. It fell like the slave's collar over his neck, finally.

"Do you mean I mustn't know the Eastwoods?" she said

"You can know them if you wish," he sneered. "But you must not expect to associate with your Granny, and your Aunt Cissie, and Lucille, if you do. I cannot have *them* contaminated. Your Granny was a faithful wife and a faithful mother, if ever one existed. She has already had one shock of shame and abomination to endure. She shall never be exposed to another."

Yvette heard it all dimly, half hearing.

"I can send a note and say you disapprove," she said dimly.

"You follow your own course of action. But remember, you have to choose between clean people, and reverence for your Granny's blameless old age, and people who are unclean in their minds and their bodies."

Again there was a silence. Then she looked at him, and her face was more puzzled than anything. But somewhere at the back of her perplexity was that peculiar calm, virgin contempt of the free-born for the base-born. He, and all the Saywells, were base-born.

"All right," she said. "I'll write and say you disapprove."

He did not answer. He was partly flattered, secretly triumphant, but abjectedly.

"I have tried to keep this from your Granny and Aunt Cissie," he said. "It need not be public property, since you choose to make your friendship clandestine."

There was a dreary silence.

"All right," she said. "I'll go and write."

And she crept out of the room.

She addressed her little note to Mrs. Eastwood. "Dear Mrs. Eastwood, Daddy doesn't approve of my coming to see you. So you will understand if we have to break it off. I'm awfully sorry—." That was all.

Yet she felt a dreary blank when she had posted her letter. She was now even afraid of her own thoughts. She wanted, now, to be held against the slender, fine-shaped breast of the gipsy. She wanted him to hold her in his arms, if only for once, for once, and comfort and confirm her. She wanted to be confirmed by him, against her father, who had only a repulsive fear of her.

And at the same time she cringed and winced, so that she could hardly walk, for fear the thought was obscene, a criminal lunacy. It seemed to wound her heels as she walked, the fear. The fear, the great cold fear of the base-born, her father, everything human and swarming. Like a great bog humanity swamped her, and she sank in, weak at the knees, filled with repulsion and fear of every person she met.

She adjusted herself, however, quite rapidly to her new conception of people. She had to live. It is useless to quarrel with one's bread and butter. And to expect a great deal out of life is puerile. So, with the rapid adaptability of the postwar generation, she adjusted herself to the new facts. Her father was what he was. He would always play up to appearances. She would do the same. She too would play up to appearances.

So, underneath the blithe, gossamer-straying insouciance, a certain hardness formed, like rock crystallising in her heart. She lost her illusions in the collapse of her sympathies. Outwardly, she seemed the same. Inwardly she was hard and detached, and, unknown to herself, revengeful.

Outwardly she remained the same. It was part of her game. While circumstances remained as they were, she must remain, at least in appearance, true to what was expected of her.

But the revengefulness came out in her new vision of people. Under the rector's apparently gallant handsomeness, she saw the weak, feeble nullity. And she despised him. Yet still, in a way, she liked him too. Feelings are so complicated.

It was Granny whom she came to detest with all her soul. That obese old woman, sitting there in her blindness like some great red-blotched fungus, her neck swallowed between her heaped-up shoulders and her rolling, ancient chins, so that she was neckless as a double potato, her Yvette really hated, with that pure, sheer hatred which is almost a joy. Her hate was so clear, that while she was feeling strong, she enjoyed it.

The old woman sat with her big, reddened face pressed a little back, her lace cap perched on her thin white hair, her stub nose still assertive, and her old mouth shut like a trap. This motherly old soul, her mouth gave her away. It always had been one of the compressed sort. But in her great age, it had gone like a toad's lipless, the jaw pressing up like the lower jaw of a trap. The look Yvette most hated, was the look of that lower jaw pressing relentlessly up, with an ancient prognathous thrust, so that the snub nose in turn was forced to press upwards, and the whole face was pressed a little back, beneath the big, wall-like forehead. The will, the ancient, toad-like obscene *will* in the old woman, was fearful, once you saw it: a toad-like self-will that was godless, and less than human! It belonged to the old, enduring race of toads, or tortoises. And it made one feel that Granny would never die. She would live on like these higher reptiles, in a state of semi-coma, forever.

Yvette dared not even suggest to her father that Granny was not perfect. He would have threatened his daughter with the lunatic asylum. That was the threat he always seemed to have up his sleeve: the lunatic asylum. Exactly as if a distaste for Granny and for that horrible house of relatives was in itself a proof of lunacy, dangerous lunacy.

Yet in one of her moods of irritable depression, she did once fling out:

"How perfectly beastly, this house is! Aunt Lucy comes, and Aunt Nell, and Aunt Alice, and they make a ring like a ring of crows, with Granny and Aunt Cissie, all lifting their skirts up and warming their legs at the fire, and shutting Lucille and me out. We're nothing but outsiders in this beastly house!"

Her father glanced at her curiously. But she managed to put a petulance into her speech, and a mere cross rudeness into her look, so that he could laugh, as at a childish tantrum. Somewhere, though, he knew that she coldly, venomously meant what she said, and he was wary of her.

Her life seemed now nothing but an irritable friction against the unsavoury household of the Saywells, in which she was immersed. She loathed the rectory with a loathing that consumed her life, a loathing so strong, that she could not really go away from the place. While it endured, she was spell-bound to it, in revulsion.

She forgot the Eastwoods again. After all! what was the revolt of the little Jewess, compared to Granny and the Saywell bunch! A husband was never more than a semicasual thing! But a family!—an awful, smelly family that would never disperse, stuck half dead round the base of a fungoid old woman! How was one to cope with that?

She did not forget the gipsy entirely. But she had no time for him. She, who was bored almost to agony, and who had nothing at all to do, she had not time to think even, seriously, of anything. Time being, after all, only the current of the soul in its flow.

She saw the gipsy twice. Once he came to the house, with things to sell. And she, watching him from the landing window, refused to go down. He saw her too, as he was putting his things back into his cart. But he too gave no sign. Being of a race that exists only to be harrying the outskirts of our society, forever hostile and living only by spoil, he was too much master to himself, and too wary, to expose himself openly to the vast and gruesome clutch of our law. He had been through the war. He had been enslaved against his will, that time.

So now, he showed himself at the rectory, and slowly, quietly busied himself at his cart outside the white gate, with that air of silent and forever-unyielding outsideness which gave him his lonely, predative grace. He knew she saw him. And she should see him unyielding, quietly hawking his copper vessels, on an old, old war-path against such as herself.

Such as herself? Perhaps he was mistaken. Her heart, in its stroke, now rang hard as his hammer upon his copper, beating against circumstances. But he struck stealthily on the outside, and she still more secretly on the inside of the establishment. She liked him. She liked the quiet, noiseless clean-cut presence of him. She liked that mysterious endurance in him, which endures in opposition, without any idea of victory. And she liked that peculiar added relentlessness, the disillusion in hostility, which belongs to after the war. Yes, if she belonged to any side, and to any clan, it was to his. Almost she could have found in her heart to go with him, and be a pariah gipsy-woman.

But she was born inside the pale. And she liked comfort, and a certain prestige. Even as a mere rector's daughter, one did have a certain prestige. And she liked that. Also she liked to chip against the pillars of the temple, from the inside. She wanted to be safe under the temple roof. Yet she enjoyed chipping fragments off the supporting pillars. Doubtless many fragments had been whittled away from the pillars of the Philistine, before Samson pulled the temple down.

"I'm not sure one shouldn't have one's fling till one is twenty-six, and then give in, and marry!"

This was Lucille's philosophy, learned from older women. Yvette was twenty-one. It meant she had five more years in which to have this precious fling. And the fling meant, at the moment, the gipsy. The marriage, at the age of twenty-six, meant Leo or Gerry.

So, a woman could eat her cake and have her bread and butter.

Yvette, pitched in gruesome, deadlocked hostility to the Saywell household, was very old and very wise: with the agedness and the wisdom of the young, which always overleaps the agedness and the wisdom of the old, or the elderly.

The second time, she met the gipsy by accident. It was March, and sunny weather, after unheard-of rain. Celandines were yellow in the hedges, and primroses among the rocks. But still there came a smell of sulphur from far-away steelworks, out of the steel-blue sky.

And yet it was spring.

Yvette was cycling slowly along by Codnor Gate, past the lime quarries, when she saw the gipsy coming away from the door of a stone cottage. His cart stood there in the road. He was returning with his brooms and copper things, to the cart.

She got down from her bicycle. As she saw him, she loved with curious tenderness, the slim lines of his body in the green jersey, the turn of his silent face. She felt she knew him better than she knew anybody on earth, even Lucille, and belonged to him, in some way, for ever.

"Have you made anything new and nice?" she asked innocently, looking at his copper things.

"I don't think," he said, glancing back at her.

The desire was still there, still curious and naked, in his eyes. But it was more remote, the boldness was diminished. There was a tiny glint, as if he might dislike her. But this dissolved again, as he saw her looking among his bits of copper and brasswork. She searched them diligently.

There was a little oval brass plate, with a queer figure like a palm-tree beaten upon it.

"I like that," she said. "How much is it?"

"What you like," he said.

This made her nervous: he seemed off-hand, almost mocking.

"I'd rather you said," she told him, looking up at him.

"You give me what you like," he said.

"No!" she said, suddenly. "If you won't tell me I won't have it."

"All right," he said. "Two shilling."

She found half-a-crown, and he drew from his pocket a handful of silver, from which he gave her her sixpence.

"The old gipsy dreamed something about you," he said, looking at her with curious, searching eyes.

"Did she!" cried Yvette, at once interested. "What was it?"

"She said: Be braver in your heart, or you lose your game. She said it this way: Be braver in your body, or your luck will leave you. And she said as well: Listen for the voice of water."

Yvette was very much impressed.

"And what does it mean?" she asked.

"I asked her," he said. "She says she don't know."

"Tell me again what it was," said Yvette.

"'Be braver in your body, or your luck will go.' And: 'Listen for the voice of water.'"

He looked in silence at her soft, pondering face. Something almost like a perfume seemed to flow from her young bosom direct to him, in a grateful connection.

"I'm to be braver in my body, and I'm to listen for the voice of water! All right!" she said. "I don't understand, but perhaps I shall."

She looked at him with clear eyes. Man or woman is made up of many selves. With one self, she loved this gipsy man. With many selves, she ignored him or had a distaste for him.

"You're not coming up to the Head no more?" he asked.

Again she looked at him absently.

"Perhaps I will," she said, "some time. Some time!"

"Spring weather!" he said, smiling faintly and glancing round at the sun. "We're going to break camp soon, and go away."

"When?" she said.

"Perhaps next week."

"Where to?"

Again he made a move with his head.

"Perhaps up north," he said.

She looked at him.

"All right!" she said. "Perhaps I *will* come up before you go, and say goodbye! to your wife and to the old woman who sent me the message."

Chapter 9

Yvette did not keep her promise. The few March days were lovely, and she let them slip. She had a curious reluctance always, towards taking action, or making any real move of her own. She always wanted someone else to make a move for her, as if she did not want to play her own game of life.

She lived as usual, went out to her friends, to parties, and danced with the undiminished Leo. She wanted to go up and say goodbye to the gipsies. She wanted to. And nothing prevented her.

On the Friday afternoon especially she wanted to go. It was sunny, and the last yellow crocuses down the drive were in full blaze, wide open, the first bees rolling in them. The Papple rushed under the stone bridge, uncannily full, nearly filling the arches. There was the scent of a mezereon tree.

And she felt too lazy, too lazy, too lazy. She strayed in the garden by the river, half dreamy, expecting something. While the gleam of spring sun lasted, she would be out of doors. Indoors Granny, sitting back like some awful old prelate, in her bulk of black silk and her white lace cap, was warming her feet by the fire, and hearing everything that Aunt Nell had to say. Friday was Aunt Nell's day. She usually came for lunch, and left after an early tea. So the mother and the large, rather common daughter, who was a widow at the age of forty, sat gossiping by the fire, while Aunt Cissie prowled in and out. Friday was the rector's day for going to town: it was also the housemaid's half day.

Yvette sat on a wooden seat in the garden, only a few feet above the bank of the swollen river, which rolled a strange, uncanny mass of water. The crocuses were passing in the ornamental beds, the grass was dark green where it was mown, the laurels looked a little brighter. Aunt Cissie appeared at the top of the porch steps, and called to ask if Yvette wanted that early cup of tea. Because of the river just below, Yvette could not hear what Aunt Cissie said, but she guessed, and shook her head. An early cup of tea, indoors, when the sun actually shone? No thanks!

She was conscious of her gipsy, as she sat there musing in the sun. Her soul had the half painful, half easing knack of leaving her, and straying away to some place, to somebody that had caught her imagination. Some days she would be all the Framleys, even though she did not go near them. Some days, she was all the time in spirit with the Eastwoods. And today it was the gipsies. She was up at their encampment in the quarry. She saw the man hammering his copper, lifting his head to look at the road; and the children playing in the horse-shelter: and the women, the gipsy's wife and the strong, elderly woman, coming home with their packs, along with the elderly man. For this afternoon, she felt intensely that *that* was home for her: the gipsy camp, the fire, the stool, the man with the hammer, the old crone.

It was part of her nature, to get these fits of yearning for some place she knew; to be in a certain place; with somebody who meant home to her. This afternoon it was the gipsy camp. And the man in the green jersey made it home to her. Just to be where he was, that was to be at home. The caravans, the brats, the other women: everything was natural to her, her home, as if she had been born there. She wondered if the gipsy was aware of her: if he could see her sitting on the stool by the fire; if he would lift his head and see her as she rose, looking at him slowly and significantly, turning towards the steps of his caravan. Did he know? Did he know?

Vaguely she looked up the steep of dark larch trees north of the house, where unseen the road climbed, going towards the Head. There was nothing, and her glance strayed down again. At the foot of the slope the river turned, thrown back harshly, ominously, against the low rocks across stream, then pouring past the garden to the bridge. It was unnaturally full, and whitey-muddy, and ponderous,

"Listen for the voice of water," she said to herself. "No need to listen for it, if the voice means the noise!"

And again she looked at the swollen river breaking angrily as it came round the bend. Above it the black-looking kitchen garden hung, and the hard-natured fruit trees. Everything was on the tilt, facing south and south-west, for the sun. Behind, above the house and the kitchen garden hung the steep little wood of withered-seeming larches. The gardener was working in the kitchen garden, high up there, by the edge of the larch-wood.

She heard a call. It was Aunt Cissie and Aunt Nell. They were on the drive, waving Goodbye! Yvette waved back. Then Aunt Cissie, pitching her voice against the waters, called:

"I shan't be long. Don't forget Granny is alone!"

"All right!" screamed Yvette rather ineffectually.

And she sat on her bench and watched the two undignified, long-coated women walk slowly over the bridge and begin the curving climb on the opposite slope, Aunt Nell carrying a sort of suit-case in which she brought a few goods for Granny and took back vegetables or whatever the rectory garden or cupboard was yielding. Slowly the two figures diminished, on the whitish, up-curving road, laboring slowly up toward Papplewick village. Aunt Cissie was going as far as the village for something.

The sun was yellowing to decline. What a pity! Oh what a pity the sunny day was going, and she would have to turn indoors, to those hateful rooms, and Granny! Aunt Cissie would be back directly: it was past five. And all the others would be arriving from town, rather irritable and tired, soon after six.

As she looked uneasily round, she heard, across the running of water, the sharp noise of a horse and cart rattling on the road hidden in the larch trees. The gardener was looking up too. Yvette turned away again, lingering, strolling by the full river a few paces, unwilling to go in; glancing up the road to see if Aunt Cissie were coming. If she saw her, she would go indoors.

She heard somebody shouting, and looked round. Down the path through the larch-trees the gipsy was bounding. The gardener, away beyond, was also running. Simultaneously she became aware of a great roar, which, before she could move, accumulated to a vast deafening snarl. The gipsy was gesticulating. She looked round, behind her.

And to her horror and amazement, round the bend of the river she saw a shaggy, tawny wavefront of water advancing like a wall of lions. The roaring sound wiped out everything. She was powerless, too amazed and wonder-struck, she wanted to see it.

Before she could think twice, it was near, a roaring cliff of water. She almost fainted with horror. She heard the scream of the gipsy, and looked up to see him bounding upon her, his black eyes starting out of his head.

"Run!" he screamed, seizing her arm.

And in the instant the first wave was washing her feet from under her, swirling, in the insane noise, which suddenly for some reason seemed like stillness, with a devouring flood over the garden. The horrible mowing of water!

The gipsy dragged her heavily, lurching, plunging, but still keeping foot-hold both of them, towards the house. She was barely conscious: as if the flood was in her soul.

There was one grass-banked terrace of the garden, near the path round the house. The gipsy clawed his way up this terrace to the dry level of the path, dragging her after him, and sprang with her past the windows to the porch steps. Before they got there, a new great surge of water came mowing, mowing trees down even, and mowed them down too.

Yvette felt herself gone in an agonising mill-race of icy water, whirled, with only the fearful grip of the gipsy's hand on her wrist. They were both down and gone. She felt a dull but stunning bruise somewhere.

Then he pulled her up. He was up, streaming forth water, clinging to the stem of the great wisteria that grew against the wall, crushed against the wall by the water. Her head was above water, he held her arm till it seemed dislocated: but she could not get her footing. With a ghastly sickness like a dream, she struggled and struggled, and could not get her feet. Only his hand was locked on her wrist.

He dragged her nearer till her one hand caught his leg. He nearly went down again. But the wisteria held him, and he pulled her up to him. She clawed at him, horribly, and got to her feet, he hanging on like a man torn in two, to the wisteria trunk.

The water was above her knees. The man and she looked into each other's ghastly streaming faces.

"Get to the steps!" he screamed.

It was only just round the corner: four strides! She looked at him: she could not go. His eyes glared on her like a tiger's, and he pushed her from him. She clung to the wall, and the water seemed to abate a little. Round the corner she staggered, but staggering, reeled and was pitched up against the cornice of the balustrade of the porch steps, the man after her.

They got on to the steps, when another roar was heard amid the roar, and the wall of the house shook. Up heaved the water round their legs again, and the gipsy had opened the hall door. In they poured with the water, reeling to the stairs. And as they did so, they saw the short but strange bulk of Granny emerge in the hall, away down from the dining-room door. She had her hands lifted and clawing, as the first water swirled round her legs, and her coffin-like mouth was opened in a hoarse scream.

Yvette was blind to everything but the stairs. Blind, unconscious of everything save the steps rising beyond the water, she clambered up like a wet, shuddering cat, in a state of unconsciousness. It was not till she was on the landing, dripping and shuddering till she could not stand erect, clinging to the banisters, while the house shook and the water raved below, that she was aware of the sodden gipsy, in paroxysms of coughing at the head of the stairs, his cap gone, his black hair over his eyes, peering between his washed-down hair at the sickening heave of water below, in the hall. Yvette, fainting, looked too, and saw Granny bob up, like a strange float, her face purple, her blind blue eyes bolting, spume hissing from her mouth. One old purple hand clawed at a banister rail, and held for a moment, showing the glint of a wedding ring.

The gipsy, who had coughed himself free and pushed back his hair, said to that awful float-like face below:

"Not good enough! Not good enough!"

With a low thud like thunder, the house was struck again, and shuttered, and a strange cracking, rattling, spitting noise began. Up heaved the water like a sea. The hand was gone, all sign of anything was gone, but upheaving water.

Yvette turned in blind unconscious frenzy, staggering like a wet cat to the upper stair-case, and climbing swiftly. It was not till she was at the door of her room that she stopped, paralysed by the sound of a sickening, tearing crash, while the house swayed.

"The house is coming down!" yelled the green-white face of the gipsy, in her face.

He glared into her crazed face.

"Where is the chimney? the back chimney?—which room? The chimney will stand—"

He glared with strange ferocity into her face, forcing her to understand. And she nodded with a strange, crazed poise, nodded quite serenely, saying: "In here! In here! It's all right."

They entered her room, which had a narrow fire-place. It was a back room with two windows, one on each side the great chimney-flue. The gipsy, coughing bitterly and trembling in every limb, went to the window to look out.

Below, between the house and the steep rise of the hill, was a wild mill-race, of water rushing with refuse, including Rover's green dog-kennel. The gipsy coughed and coughed, and gazed down blankly. Tree after tree went down, mown by the water, which must have been ten feet deep.

Shuddering and pressing his sodden arms on his sodden breast, a look of resignation on his livid face, he turned to Yvette. A fearful tearing noise tore the house, then there was a deep, watery explosion. Something had gone down, some part of the house, the floor heaved and wavered beneath them. For some moments both were suspended, stupefied. Then he roused.

"Not good enough! Not good enough! This will stand. This here will stand. See that chimney! like a tower. Yes! All right! All right. You take your clothes off and go to bed. You'll die of the cold."

"It's all right! It's quite all right!" she said to him, sitting on a chair and looking up into his face with her white, insane little face, round which the hair was plastered.

"No!" he cried. "No! Take your things off and I rub you with this towel. I rub myself. If the house falls then die warm. If it don't fall, then live, not die of pneumonia."

Coughing, shuddering violently, he pulled up his jersey hem and wrestled with all his shuddering, cold-cracked might, to get off his wet, tight jersey.

"Help me!" he cried, his face muffled.

She seized the edge of the jersey, obediently, and pulled with all her might. The garment came over his head, and he stood in his braces.

"Take your things off! Rub with this towel!" he commanded ferociously, the savageness of the war on him. And like a thing obsessed, he pushed himself out of his trousers, and got out of his wet, clinging shirt, emerging slim and livid, shuddering in every fibre with cold and shock.

He seized a towel, and began quickly to rub his body, his teeth chattering like plates rattling together. Yvette dimly saw it was wise. She tried to get out of her dress. He pulled the horrible wet death-gripping thing off her, then, resuming his rubbing, went to the door, tip-toeing on the wet floor.

There he stood, naked, towel in hand, petrified. He looked west, towards where the upper landing window had been, and was looking into the sunset, over an insane sea of waters, bristling with uptorn trees and refuse. The end corner of the house, where porch had been, and the stairs, had gone. The wall had fallen, leaving the floor sticking out. The stairs had gone.

Motionless, he watched the water. A cold wind blew in upon him. He clenched his rattling teeth with a great effort of will, and turned into the room again, closing the door.

Yvette, naked, shuddering so much that she was sick, was trying to wipe herself dry.

"All right!" he cried. "All right! The water don't rise no more! All right!"

With his towel he began to rub her, himself shaking all over, but holding her gripped by the shoulder, and slowly, numbedly rubbing her tender body, even trying to rub up into some dryness the pitiful hair of her small head. Suddenly he left off.

"Better lie in the bed," he commanded, "I want to rub myself."

His teeth went snap-snap-snap-snap, in great snaps, cutting off his words. Yvette crept shaking and semi-conscious into her bed. He, making strained efforts to hold himself still and rub himself warm, went again to the north window, to look out.

The water had risen a little. The sun had gone down, and there was a reddish glow. He rubbed his hair into a black, wet tangle, then paused for breath, in a sudden access of shuddering, then looked out again, then rubbed again on his breast, and began to cough afresh, because of the water he had swallowed. His towel was red: he had hurt himself somewhere: but he felt nothing.

There was still the strange huge noise of water, and the horrible bump of things bumping against the walls. The wind was rising with sundown, cold and hard. The house shook with explosive thuds, and weird, weird frightening noises came up.

A terror creeping over his soul, he went again to the door. The wind, roaring with the waters, blew in as he opened it. Through the awesome gap in the house he saw the world, the waters, the chaos of horrible waters, the twilight, the perfect new moon high above the sunset, a faint thing, and clouds pushing dark into the sky, on the cold, blustery wind.

Clenching his teeth again, fear mingling with resignation, or fatalism, in his soul, he went into the room and closed the door, picking up her towel to see if it were drier than his own, and less blood-stained, again rubbing his head, and going to the window.

He turned away, unable to control his spasms of shivering. Yvette had disappeared right under the bed-clothes, and nothing of her was visible but a shivering mound under the white quilt. He laid his hand on this shivering mound, as if for company. It did not stop shivering.

"All right!" he said. "All right! Water's going down."

She suddenly uncovered her head and peered out at him from a white face. She peered into his greenish, curiously calm face, semi-conscious. His teeth were chattering unheeded, as he gazed down at her, his black eyes still full of the fire of life and a certain vagabond calm of fatalistic resignation.

"Warm me!" she moaned, with chattering teeth. "Warm me! I shall die of shivering."

A terrible convulsion went through her curled-up white body, enough indeed to rupture her and cause her to die.

The gipsy nodded, and took her in his arms, and held her in a clasp like a vice, to still his own shuddering. He himself was shuddering fearfully, and only semi-conscious. It was the shock.

The vice-like grip of his arms round her seemed to her the only stable point in her consciousness. It was a fearful relief to her heart, which was strained to bursting. And though his body, wrapped round her strange and lithe and powerful, like tentacles, rippled with shuddering as an electric current, still the rigid tension of the muscles that held her clenched steadied them both, and gradually the sickening violence of the shuddering, caused by shock, abated, in his body first, then in hers, and the warmth revived between them. And as it roused, their tortured, semi-conscious minds became unconscious, they passed away into sleep.

Chapter 10

The sun was shining in heaven before men were able to get across the Papple with ladders. The bridge was gone. But the flood had abated, and the house, that leaned forwards as if it were making a stiff bow to the stream, stood now in mud and wreckage, with a great heap of fallen masonry and debris at the south-west corner. Awful were the gaping mouths of rooms!

Inside, there was no sign of life. But across-stream the gardener had come to reconnoitre, and the cook appeared, thrilled with curiosity. She had escaped from the back door and up through the larches to the high-road, when she saw the gipsy bound past the house: thinking he was coming to murder somebody. At the little top gate she had found his cart standing. The gardener had led the horse away to the Red Lion up at Darley, when night had fallen.

This the men from Papplewick learned when at last they got across the stream with ladders, and to the back of the house. They were nervous, fearing a collapse of the building, whose front was all undermined and whose back was choked up. They gazed with horror at the silent shelves of the rector's rows of books, in his torn-open study; at the big brass bedstead of Granny's room, the bed so deep and comfortably made, but one brass leg of the bed-stead perched tentatively over the torn void; at the wreckage of the maid's room upstairs. The housemaid and the cook wept. Then a man climbed in cautiously through a smashed kitchen window, into the jungle and morass of the ground floor. He found the body of the old woman: or at least he saw her foot, in its flat black slipper, muddily protruding from a mud-heap of debris. And he fled.

The gardener said he was sure that Miss Yvette was not in the house. He had seen her and the gipsy swept away. But the policeman insisted on a search, and the Framley boys rushing up at last, the ladders were roped together. Then the whole party set up a loud yell. But without result. No answer from within.

A ladder was up, Bob Framley climbed, smashed a window, and clambered into Aunt Cissie's room. The perfect homely familiarity of everything terrified him like ghosts. The house might go down any minute.

They had just got the ladder up to the top floor, when men came running from Darley, saying the old gipsy had been to the Red Lion for the horse and cart, leaving word that his son had seen Yvette at the top of the house. But by that time the policeman was smashing the window of Yvette's room.

Yvette, fast asleep, started from under the bed-clothes with a scream, as the glass flew. She clutched the sheets round her nakedness. The policeman uttered a startled yell, which he converted into a cry of: Miss Yvette! Miss Yvette! He turned round on the ladder, and shouted to the faces below.

"Miss Yvette's in bed!—in bed!"

And he perched there on the ladder, an unmarried man, clutching the window in peril, not knowing what to do.

Yvette sat up in bed, her hair in a matted tangle, and stared with wild eyes, clutching up the sheets at her naked breast. She had been so very fast asleep, that she was still not there.

The policeman, terrified at the flabby ladder, climbed into the room, saying:

"Don't be frightened, Miss! Don't you worry any more about it. You're safe now."

And Yvette, so dazed, thought he meant the gipsy. Where was the gipsy? This was the first thing in her mind. Where was her gipsy of this world's-end night?

He was gone! He was gone! And a policeman was in the room! A policeman!

She rubbed her hand over her dazed brow.

"If you'll get dressed, Miss, we can get you down to safe ground. The house is likely to fall. I suppose there's nobody in the other rooms?"

He stepped gingerly into the passage, and gazed in terror through the torn-out end of the house, and far-off saw the rector coming down in a motor-car, on the sunlit hill.

Yvette, her face gone numb and disappointed, got up quickly, closing the bed-clothes, and looked at herself a moment, then opened her drawers for clothing. She dressed herself, then looked in a mirror, and saw her matted hair with horror. Yet she did not care. The gipsy was gone, anyhow.

Her own clothes lay in a sodden heap. There was a great sodden place on the carpet where his had been, and two blood-stained filthy towels. Otherwise there was no sign of him.

She was tugging at her hair when the policeman tapped at her door. She called him to come in. He saw with relief that she was dressed and in her right senses.

"We'd better get out of the house as soon as possible, Miss," he re-iterated. "It might fall any minute."

"Really!" said Yvette calmly. "Is it as bad as that?"

There were great shouts. She had to go to the window. There, below, was the rector, his arms wide open, tears streaming down his face.

"I'm perfectly all right, Daddy!" she said, with the calmness of her contradictory feelings. She would keep the gipsy a secret from him. At the same time, tears ran down her face.

"Don't you cry, Miss, don't you cry! The rector's lost his mother, but he's thanking his stars to have his daughter. We all thought you were gone as well, we did that!"

"Is Granny drowned?" said Yvette.

"I'm afraid she is, poor lady!" said the policeman, with a grave face.

Yvette wept away into her hanky, which she had had to fetch from a drawer.

"Dare you go down that ladder, Miss?" said the policeman.

Yvette looked at the sagging depth of it, and said promptly to herself: No! Not for anything!—But then she remembered the gipsy's saying: "Be braver in the body."

"Have you been in all the other rooms?" she said, in her keeping, turning to the policeman.

"Yes, Miss! But you was the only person in the house, you know, save the old lady. Cook got away in time, and Lizzie was up at her mother's. It was only you and the poor old lady we was fretting about. Do you think you dare go down that ladder?"

"Oh, yes!" said Yvette with indifference. The gipsy was gone anyway.

And now the rector in torment watched his tall, slender daughter slowly stepping backwards down the sagging ladder, the policeman, peering heroically from the smashed window, holding the ladder's top ends.

At the foot of the ladder Yvette appropriately fainted in her father's arms, and was borne away with him, in the car, by Bob, to the Framley home. There the poor Lucille, a ghost of ghosts, wept with relief till she had hysterics, and even Aunt Cissie cried out among her tears: "Let the old be taken and the young spared! Oh I *can't* cry for the Mater, now Yvette is spared!"

And she wept gallons.

The flood was caused by the sudden bursting of the great reservoir, up in Papple Highdale, five miles from the rectory. It was found out later that an ancient, perhaps even a Roman mine tunnel, unsuspected, undreamed of, beneath the reservoir dam, had collapsed, undermining the whole dam. That was why the Papple had been, for the last day, so uncannily full. And then the dam had burst.

The rector and the two girls stayed on at the Framleys', till a new home could be found. Yvette did not attend Granny's funeral. She stayed in bed.

Telling her tale, she only told how the gipsy had got her inside the porch, and she had crawled to the stairs out of the water. It was known that he had escaped: the old gipsy had said so, when he fetched the horse and cart from the Red Lion. Yvette could tell little. She was vague, confused, she seemed hardly to remember anything. But that was just like her.

It was Bob Framley who said:

"You know, I think that gipsy deserves a medal."

The whole family was suddenly struck.

"Oh, we *ought* to thank him!" cried Lucille.

The rector himself went with Bob in the car. But the quarry was deserted. The gipsies had lifted camp and gone, no one knew whither.

And Yvette, lying in bed, moaned in her heart: Oh, I love him! I love him! I love him!—The grief over him kept her prostrate. Yet practically, she too was acquiescent in the fact of his disappearance. Her young soul knew the wisdom of it.

But after Granny's funeral, she received a little letter, dated from some unknown place.

"Dear Miss, I see in the paper you are all right after your ducking, as is the same with me. I hope I see you again one day, maybe at Tideswell cattle fair, or maybe we come that way again. I come that day to say goodbye! and I never said it, well, the water give no time, but I live in hopes. Your obdt. servant Joe Boswell."

And only then she realised that he had a name.

CPSIA information can be obtained
at www.ICGtesting.com
Printed in the USA
LVHW061410011222
734355LV00015B/813

9 781805 470311